Accidental Us

A SMALL-TOWN ENEMIES-TO-LOVERS ROMANTIC COMEDY

ZOEY LOCKE

WITH

TABI RYAN

This is a work of fiction. All characters, organizations, and events portrayed in this novel are either products of the author's imagination or are used fictionally.

ISBN: 978-1-963546-29-3

Formatted with Vellum

Contents

CHAPTER 1
Unlucky Day
GINA

I'm ALREADY LATE for work and dreading the inevitable reaction from my boss, ex-celebrity chef Randy Thorn, who's also a thorn in my side. That's why I pull into the first empty parking space I see and hit the brakes with more force than necessary. I'm just frustrated that I'm late again. Clutching the steering wheel tightly, I visualize the disapproving look on Randy's way too handsome face. I really, really hate that he's so good-looking. He could choose to be anywhere in the restaurant— the kitchen, the office, even the bathroom—yet I'm certain he'll be at the counter, checking the time as I walk in.

After a mournful groan, I look at the clock on

the stereo. It's 1:17 p.m. I should have been here seventeen minutes ago. Sighing, I mutter to myself. "Dang it." There's nothing to do now but face the music. So I snatch my purse off the passenger seat and swing open the door of my ten-year-old, weather-beaten Honda Civic. Then I feel and hear it as the jarring noise of metal grinding against metal reverberates through me.

Horrified by what I've just done, I let out a sharp gasp, my hand flying to cover my mouth. "Oh no, no, no!" Can my luck get any worse today? This morning, I overslept by an hour after not hearing my alarm, missing the first half of class and the crucial knife skills exam. Fortunately, Chef Blasingame agreed to let me take the test in a brief fifteen-minute window after class, but that bit of grace extended to me has made me later for work than usual. It now seems clear that luck has wholly deserted me today.

Yet dwelling on this recent mishap is not an option. I get moving, scrambling out of my car to assess the damage. *Yikes.* The edge of my car door has carved a nasty gouge through the paint and metal of someone's bright-red Mercedes Benz.

"Great," I grumble under my breath. My eyes

sweep the parking lot in search of the car's owner, even though I really don't have time for this. But my scan is fruitless. Even though nearly every spot is taken, there's nobody out here but me. Why, oh why, couldn't my car have nicked that tiny, less expensive vehicle at the end of the row instead? I wish I could ignore this. I shudder to think how much this is going to set me back.

Thinking on my feet, I dig through my purse and find a pen and an old business card from Jack of All Tires. I quickly sketch an arrow on it and jot down, "Sorry about the door. Find me at the register. Will pay. - Gina E." I'm not entirely sure how I'll manage to pay the bill, but I'm willing to try. I slide the card under the wiper blade on the driver's side and dash across the lot, making a beeline for the café.

Once inside, I'm almost immediately swept up in the vibrant chatter of our bustling dining room. This place is a hit for a reason: the food is simply out of this world.

"You're late," Randy grumbles. The grouchy chef's culinary magic is the secret behind the restaurant's newfound popularity. He's positioned right where I knew he would be and doesn't even bother looking up from the work he's pretending to do.

"I know," I barely whisper as I dart past him, heading straight for the staff locker room. I can sense Randy's glare boring into me, loaded with silent reprimand. It seems like making my life more difficult than usual is his favorite pastime.

The locker room is filled with the inviting aroma of fresh-baked bread, smoked meats, and savory sauces. I inhale deeply, relishing the heavenly scent. The smell almost makes me forget I'm working for a tyrant.

We're not assigned lockers, but since we're all creatures of habit, I open the one I always use. While rummaging through the metal box for my apron, my deodorant and lipstick tumble out, clattering onto the wooden bench and then to the floor.

"Gosh, I'm such a mess," I mumble, aware that every passing second is crucial. Randy is likely blowing his top by now.

Quickly, I pick up the fallen items. My locker is crammed with so many books that there's hardly space for anything else. I'm back in school. This time I'm learning the culinary arts. I'm enrolled in an intensive program that boasts it will make me a professional chef in just eighteen months. I'm sixteen months in, and I would say that I've come a long way since the beginning. Most of my favorite classes are for baking, though. I'm not sure I've taken to cooking more than I have to whipping up delectable breads and desserts. I love the art of baking more than anything.

Suddenly, the door swings open, and I instinctively straighten up. Randy strides in. His imposing physique and striking good looks command my attention.

"I didn't anticipate you being late every day after we discussed your plans for school," he says, his tone so disapproving.

After finding my apron, I slam the locker shut. "Neither did I," I reply, meeting his glare with defiance.

I watch the show as he widens his stance and folds his arms—his favorite pose. And really, you know, I should not be attracted to how he looks right now. That's why I make a concerted effort to divert my gaze from his chiseled biceps and the tattoo on the front of his forearm, which I really, *really* like a lot.

"Why should I continue supporting you when

you're constantly late?" His words jolt me from a momentary lapse of judgment.

As usual, when we're locking horns, I mirror his posture, folding my arms and meeting his gaze with a snarl. "Are you seriously asking me that?"

"Yes, I am." As usual, his tone drips with arrogance.

What a jerk. I roll my eyes dismissively. "Well, you didn't seem to have much of a problem with my tardiness after my muffins and tarts sold in record numbers."

Yes, indeed. A few months back, one of the bakers abruptly left in the middle of his shift. I stayed late to finish his work, but instead of following his recipes, I used my own. For the next three weeks, customers couldn't get enough of them. Fortunately, Randy set aside his pride, albeit reluctantly, and asked for my recipe. Now my pastries have earned a permanent spot on the menu.

"Beginner's luck," he snaps dismissively.

I gasp, offended. "Are you really this big of a jerk?"

Randy shakes his head and massages the bridge of his nose as if my tardiness is the ultimate inconvenience. "Damn it, Gina. Could you just stop being late from now on?"

I open my mouth, poised to stick to my guns.

"Because," he continues, "I've shown you a lot of leniency."

Numerous thoughts race through my mind. One of them is urging me to calm down and be rational and, by all means, avoid the ultimate power struggle with this guy. Because surprisingly, he's right. Despite his abrasive manner, he has been remarkably tolerant of the fact that I'm hardly ever on time for my shift.

There's also something only my best friend Naomi knows about us, and that is that despite Randy's difficult nature, we've had sex. And we've done it more than once, twice… well, I stopped counting after six or seven times. What's my excuse? Simply put, Randy is undeniably hot, and sometimes, even I can't resist him. Although, in hindsight, each time we succumb to our desires, I feel regret. Well, at least a pinch of regret… Or maybe a grain of regret… Okay, fine. I hate to admit it, but I feel no regret at all.

Maybe that's why, at this very moment, my heart is pounding like crazy. We're locked in a stare-down. The atmosphere in the room feels charged, almost as if it has become electrified. All I can think about is the desire to feel his sensually swollen lips pressed against mine. Yes, Randy possesses the most enticing mouth. Making out with him is, unfortunately, highly enjoyable. It infuriates me how irresistibly sexy he is.

The door swings open abruptly, snapping me back to reality. Rita, a coworker, peers into the room. Her inquisitive gaze shifts between Randy and me, and suspicion flickers in her eyes as if she suspects she's interrupted something heated between us. She's asked me on several occasions if there's something going on between Randy and me. I hate denying it. Rita is one of my good friends. But I will never tell anyone who works here what Randy and I get up to when left alone. And I mean *never*.

"Jeremy's at the register, asking for you," she says. Her eyebrows knit together suspiciously.

"All right, tell him—" Randy begins.

"No, not you," Rita interrupts. "Gina."

Randy's frown deepens. "What does Jeremy want with Gina?"

Confusion swirls in my mind as I shake my head. "Who's Jeremy?"

"He says you left a card on his windshield," Rita explains.

"Oh." I sigh heavily. "That Jeremy."

"My cousin," Randy adds.

A groan escapes from deep within my belly. *Randy's cousin? I dented Randy's cousin's very expensive car?* Suddenly, I feel nauseated. Nope, this is not my lucky day.

CHAPTER 2

Old Habits Don't Die

GINA

I FEEL like I'm being forced to walk the plank as I make my way to the main dining room. I could almost throw up. I would rather do that than face this guy. Yet my steps halt when I catch sight of the man standing in front of the cash register. That has to be him. He's a tall, striking ginger with undeniable appeal. He's the kind of guy who would drive a shiny red Mercedes Benz, like the one I left my mark on. With a hand on my stomach to steady myself, I send up prayer, hoping he's nothing like his uptight cousin.

It's time to put on a show. I summon my brightest smile, re-straighten my posture, and stride confidently toward Mr. Moneybags, arm outstretched. "Hi, I'm Gina." My aim is to charm him into going easy on me. I've tried that tactic with Randy to no avail.

Mr. Moneybags greets me with a firm handshake. "Nice to meet you, Gina. You did some serious damage to my door." His direct approach reminds me so much of Randy—straight to the point with no finesse. They're definitely cousins.

"She doesn't have all day to chitchat, Jer," Randy interjects, coming up behind the counter with his usual briskness.

I sigh, increasingly frustrated by the entire ordeal. I wish Randy had stayed in the back. His presence only complicates things further.

"We can exchange insurance information," I suggest, trying to steer the conversation toward the quickest resolution possible.

Jeremy, or "Jer" as Randy refers to him, locks his gaze on mine. His face lights up with a megawatt smile. "What do you say about this?"

I tilt my head curiously. "About what?"

He folds his arms across his broad chest and adopts a stance reminiscent of Randy's. "A proposition," he states firmly.

I'm cautious but intrigued, especially since his tone suggests this proposition won't cost me a fortune. "What kind of proposition?" I ask, eager to hear more.

"I'm willing to forgive and forget the damage to my car if you agree to go out with me on…" his eyes narrow as if he's making an assessment. "… three dates."

I yank my head back, stunned. *Why would he…?* Only now do I see the spark of attraction in his eyes. Quickly, I glance at Randy, who is watching us as if he's curious to know my answer. Three dates are a lot. Then again, Jeremy's car looks pretty new, and I imagine the damage I did will cost more than a couple of bucks to fix. On top of that, he isn't bad on the eyes.

But then there's Randy to consider. I mean, when we're left alone, we're still unable to keep our hands and bodies to ourselves.

Now Randy folds his arms in that arrogant way of his. Grinning and amused, he waits to hear my answer.

"Why three dates?" I finally ask Jeremy.

Jeremy flashes another gorgeous lopsided grin. "Because you've done three dates' worth of damage."

I shake my head, teetering on the brink of refusal. Then I steal a glance at my coworkers, Rita and Sarah, who are nodding, encouraging me to accept Jeremy's proposal. But something about it feels odd. It's as if he's attempting to purchase my company, and that doesn't sit well with me. I could simply borrow the money from my parents.

Before I can make a decision, Randy interjects in his usual grumbling voice. "Jeremy, that's enough. Back off my employee! We're not paying her to socialize."

I grunt, rolling my eyes. Could he stop being a jerk for five minutes?

"Hey, we're striking a deal here," Jeremy counters, maintaining his charismatic smile.

"No deal," Randy says. "I'll pay for the damage."

My insides erupt with indignation. "No way!" I exclaim, shaking my head adamantly. "I'll take the dates. There's no way I'm owing you a dime."

Randy's jaw drops open.

I don't care that he's speechless. The last thing I want is to give him more leverage over me. Owing him money would give him too much power, and that's exactly why I decide to accept Jeremy's deal.

8 HOURS LATER

Randy only lingered at the front of the shop long enough to become irritated by my interaction with Jeremy. I haven't seen much of him since the lunch rush and after-work crowds thinned out. It's not like I've been actively looking for him—or perhaps I have. I hate how my chest fills with a swarm of butterflies every time I unexpectedly catch a glimpse of him. I must be crazy, feeling this way about him. My man-picking instincts must be way off.

Thankfully, the café is now closed. Exhausted, I finish wiping down tables. It has been an exceptionally long day. Usually, I rise at 6 a.m. Wednesday morning for a 7 a.m. class. Lately, I've been burning the midnight oil, studying and experimenting with new recipes. Baking has always been my forte, but I find cooking over the stove to be more challenging. I work hard because I want my grades to reflect how much I love the culinary arts.

"Hey, Gina!"

I send my tired gaze across the room. Pete, the second-shift baker, stands at the register with his coat on and keys in hand.

"Yeah?" I ask with a yawn.

"Are you closing tonight?"

"Yep."

He grins, visibly relieved. "Could you do me a favor and prepare the dough for the next few hours? My daughter has an event tonight, and the kid is counting on me being there."

If history is any indication, Pete already knows my answer. Plus, I'm grinning from ear to ear, thrilled to be asked to do the task I enjoy most.

"Sure, but is Randy around?" I ask, anxiety fluttering in my chest. He would undoubtedly have an issue with me taking extra time to prepare the dough instead of immediately closing the register and getting ready for the morning shift.

I only work in the kitchen on days when Randy isn't here. When I made my famous blueberry and strawberry stuffed puffs, which have since been added to the menu, Randy was absent for two weeks. If he were around, that would never have happened.

Pete is already heading for the exit when he answers. "I haven't seen him all day. Can you do it?"

I twist my lips nervously. After agreeing to go on three dates with Randy's cousin, I don't want any more trouble with Randy. But there's no way I can say no, especially when Pete assures me he'll be back within three hours. Besides, he's practically out the door already.

Time flies as I measure ingredients, adding my personal touches to the batch while making dough. When I get into baking mode, there's no stopping me, and before long, I'm whipping up batter for muffins. Pete must've known I would do that, too; he's lined up the dry ingredients I need on the counter. We both know I make the best raspberry vanilla swirl cro-muffins, which are a cross between a croissant and a muffin.

"You're still here?" a voice asks.

I jump, startled, immediately recognizing the voice. Then I quickly turn my attention toward the doorway to see Randy.

"Pete has a thing tonight. I'm just helping," I explain, relieved to have just placed the final batch of muffin tins in the refrigerator. I pull the tie on my apron, loosening it. "I know I'm supposed to close tonight, so I'll go out and count the register."

Randy appears just as exhausted as I am as he saunters into the kitchen on slightly bowed legs. He is the mere definition of poetry in motion. And I really loathe that is the thought that's in my head.

"I've already done it," he says in a husky and sultry voice.

My eyebrows raise, but not because I'm surprised. Randy is a workhorse. He'll get the task done first and ask questions later. It's one of his most admirable qualities, actually. However, I wait for the other shoe to drop, the part where he lectures me about doing my job before I amuse myself in the kitchen without his consent.

Instead, he sighs as he puts on an apron. My eyes gravitate to his broad chest, accentuated as he wraps the ties around his waist. His body looks perfect. My best friend, Naomi Sutters, always says he looks like Clark Kent, Superman's alter ego. I would never admit it out loud, but I think Randy is cuter. He could be a Hollywood movie star. All of his facial features are perfectly placed, and he has just the right amount of everything—cheekbones, chin, forehead, nose, and those sexy bedroom eyes. I love watching his face whenever we have sex. If only he weren't so difficult 99.9 percent of the time.

He hasn't reprimanded me yet, though, which means it might be best to leave while we're still on speaking terms. I raise my arms to stretch as I yawn. "Well, I'm done here, so…"

Randy tilts his head ever so slightly as he opens a container of flour. "Could you stick around a little longer?"

We're gazing intently at each other. The way his eyes smolder makes my heart thump like persistent thunder. That's all it takes for Randy to convey that he wants to explore this magnificent flame that ignites between us when we're alone, a flame that can't be quelled. As usual, my brain is shouting, "No! Go! Leave now!" One day, this thing that we do, our little secret, is going to hurt very badly. But every other part of me wants to stick around for more.

"For what?" I finally ask, trying hard to put up a defense against the power he has over me.

"Let me make something for you." His tone is syrupy, and I'm lapping up its sweet flavor.

That familiar feeling lingers in the air. This is how it always starts between us.

I search beyond his shoulders and out into the unlit hallway. "Are we the only ones here?"

Randy is already measuring flour and dropping it into the bowl of the electronic mixer. In addition to his normal chef's ego, he's so sure of himself. It's as if he knows I've already chosen to stay and allow our future to unfold in life's most pleasurable way. "Yes," he says without looking at me.

This is my last chance to get out. I should leave. I really should. But instead I walk over to stand beside him. "What are you making?" He smells so good. Did he douse himself in cologne since this morning?

He glances at me with a gorgeous half-smile. "It's a secret."

"Why are you making secrets for me tonight?"

He looks at me, maintaining his lopsided grin, which sends a thrill through me. "Why not?"

"Because earlier in the break room, you weren't that nice."

"You were late."

"You know I have school, Randy, which by the way, makes me more able to help in the kitchen."

He's measuring a teaspoon of vanilla. I go to the rack and retrieve the brown bottle of vanilla butter emulsion that I made a few days ago.

"I'm doing free baker's work." I twist the cap off the emulsion. "Use a teaspoon of this too."

"No." He cracks three eggs like he can give a master class in egg cracking.

"Yes." I pour a teaspoon of the dense liquid into the batter.

Randy flips the mixer off. "Why are you so difficult?"

I swipe a finger through his batter and hold it in front of his scrumptious lips. "I could ask the same question."

We're tumbling deeper into each other's stare. Every part of me throbs for more of Randy, especially when his mouth consumes my finger and his tongue gently glides around the tip of it.

That's all it takes. It happens like a fire erupting out of thin air. Lightning strikes. I'm contained by his fit arms. All day, I've wanted to taste his mouth, and now I am indulging in his kiss. It's making me dizzy with desire. Our hands, mouths, and movements are instinctual. We've done this so many times before, we know what to do. The clothes that restrict us from being closer are off. Suddenly, Randy lifts my feet off the floor and sets me on the counter. His strong hand presses upward against my thigh.

I shouldn't.

We shouldn't.

But the warmth of his mouth and the force of his lips are so addictive. My thoughts lose the battle against his intractable pull. Suddenly, I gasp, feeling him deep inside me. Soon, all I want is to merge into Randy Thorn.

And then, I moan, experiencing the pure bliss of making love to a perfectionist.

FIFTEEN... MAYBE TWENTY MINUTES LATER

Randy and I are putting the finishing touches on buttoning our shirts and zipping our pants. As usual, we've arrived at the point where we can barely look each other in the eyes.

"Oh, and about Jeremy," Randy says, collecting my full attention.

We stare at each other. My heart swells, full of the strong emotions of after-sex.

"What about him?" I'm barely able to voice.

"I can pay for the damage to his car. You don't have to go out with him."

I'm already shaking my head. Even after we've just gotten as close as people can humanly get, I still don't want to be beholden to the side of Randy that can be a complete jerk. But arguing with him about it is not the postcoital behavior I want to engage in right now.

"I'll be fine," I say, waving off his concern. But then another thought comes to mind. "Unless he's someone I should be wary about?"

"No, no," he says, shaking his head adamantly. "It's not that."

"Then what is it?"

His eyebrows become animated, as if he's battling inner turmoil. For a moment, I almost think Randy is jealous. Surely, he's not jealous. He has made it very clear that this thing between us is just sex. And I've conveyed the same thing to him.

I remember this instance last year at our Christmas party, in front of everybody, he said, "I can't wait to see the guy Gina ends up with. I bet he'll be…" And then he raised his eyebrows.

"He'll be what?" I snapped, determined not to let him off the hook.

He bounced his eyebrows again.

I was steaming. We had already done the deed about twice then. He was Mr. Mixed Signals then and still is now.

"To hell with it," he finally says. "I just know he's not your type."

I want to say, "Why do I care if he's my type or

not? I'm just paying off an easy debt." But I still don't want to bicker with Randy after sex, so I just say, "Okay. I'll keep that in mind."

After a moment, he turns his back on me and walks out, leaving me staring at the empty space he leaves behind, trying to figure out what I'm feeling right now. The way we did it tonight was different. We could hardly keep our mouths off each other. Every caress, squeeze, and rub could be felt deeply.

Could that have been something more? Like love? Is that why Randy is warning me about his cousin?

Then I shake my head. It couldn't have been love. I could never love Randy, and he could never love me. We're oil and water—the furthest of binaries, existing on two opposite ends of the spectrum.

No. Whatever emotions we have for each other don't penetrate beneath the surface. I push thoughts of him away. Instead, I focus on the idea of a shower, my bed, and the deeply needed sleep awaiting me. With that in mind, I clock out of my shift for the day.

CHAPTER 3

Debt Date

GINA

As I lie in bed, tracing the delicate crack in the ceiling with my weary gaze, my eyelids begin to feel impossibly heavy. What a whirlwind of emotions today has been, and the gust has followed me into the night. As I drift softly into the embrace of sleep, the memory of Randy's kiss lingers. I touch my lips and feel the fleeting echo of passion flutter through me. It's curious how swiftly the fiery moments shared between lovers dissolves into the ether of our minds. At first, there's this electric spark of attraction that ignites an exhilarating rush. Then in the heat of connection, we soar, touched by euphoria. But as quickly as it ignites, the flame dims, leaving those shared moments to gently recede into the tapestry of our past.

With Randy, it's a dance of shadows—intense and captivating, yet elusive, slipping through my fingers like whispers of smoke. I can never seem to hold on to him, to carry the essence of us beyond the now. And in these quiet, introspective moments, I find myself pondering—do I even want to? Do I yearn to anchor him, to weave him into the fabric of my tomorrows?

Honestly, I don't know much about Randy except that he almost became a famous chef in New York City before something big happened. We've never talked about what went wrong, and we've never really been on an actual date. People say Randy doesn't do dates, even though lots of folks have tried to catch his eye. He's pretty popular. It makes me wonder if I am the only one he's doing.

The idea that I might not be his only secret hookup bothers me a lot. I toss and turn in bed, feeling all kinds of upset. *That's it.* I decide here and now that Randy and I are done. It is time to move on.

But even as I decide we're done, I'm not sure I believe it.

My phone rings, pulling me out of my reverie. I flip over onto my stomach and reach for my device.

I'm actually glad for the distraction. My thoughts were making decisions that I'm not ready to contend with yet.

"Hello?" I answer, probably sounding too excited.

"Is this Gina?" asks a man on the other end.

I can't tell who it is, which makes me pause. "Yes. Who's this?"

"Jeremy. The guy you're dating." He chuckles.

I, too, can't help but laugh. This has to be a joke. "Yeah, right." I sit up against my headboard to give this conversation my full attention.

"I hope I'm not calling too late. I just wanted to check to see if you're free tomorrow night."

He sounds so cheery, as I stifle a yawn. This guy moves fast.

"You really don't waste time, do you?" I remark, half-amused, half-impressed.

His laughter comes through the phone, and it reminds me so much of Randy's that I suddenly feel more awake.

"Not when the person who owes me is as pretty as you." His flirting is obvious, but adorable.

I blurt out a laugh. "Cute." I'm not entirely charmed, but I am nevertheless intrigued. Right now, the idea of using one of my precious two nights off for what I'm calling a "debt date" doesn't thrill me. Yet part of me reasons that the sooner I start, the sooner it will all be behind me. "I work until five tomorrow. Can you pick me up at the Calypso then?" I find myself already wishing I would've just asked my parents for the money.

THE NEXT DAY

After Jeremy's call, my mind kept considering ways I could become comfortable with accepting Randy's proposal to pay for the car damage until I fell asleep. I can't remember what I concluded; a deep sleep erased those thoughts. Yesterday was a tough Wednesday, but Thursday is a bit lighter. I only had my knife skills class in the morning, and my shift started at 11 a.m.

I arrived at the diner just in time, one minute before I was scheduled to start. Like clockwork, Randy was there, casually leaning on the counter, pretending he wasn't keeping an eye out for my arrival. But as soon as I walked in, he quickly told Sarah, with a gentle touch on her shoulder, that she could take her break once I took over the register, which would be in about five minutes.

I rolled my eyes at his behavior. That is typical Randy, acting all distant and cool after we hook up. Honestly, it's just so annoying, this aftermath of us giving into our yearning. I can barely stand it.

Despite feeling a bit embarrassed by what was churning in my thoughts, I couldn't help but wonder if Sarah might be another one of Randy's secret conquests. But that thought quickly went down in the flames of remorse and reproach. Sarah is totally smitten with her boyfriend, Dan. They're one of those couples who just get each other, always finishing each other's sentences. They're inseparable, two peas in a pod, and not the type to cheat on their significant other. So, no, Sarah definitely isn't involved with Randy.

Yet true to form, post our latest encounter, Randy has been keeping his distance all day. Part of me misses seeing him around, but it's also a relief not to have him hovering, ready to pounce on any mistake I make.

Now the afternoon has faded away, my shift is over, and I've slipped into my date outfit: skinny jeans, a black scoop-neck T-shirt, a leather biker jacket, and booties with a modest heel. I'm aiming for a look that is both stylish and laid-back.

As for Jeremy, I'm not sure what to expect. Could I end up more physically and sexually attracted to him than Randy? I don't know yet, but I'm open to finding out. After all, Randy hasn't exactly been clear about what he wants from me beyond the obvious. Keeping my options open seems like the best plan for now.

"Looks like your date's here." Randy's voice comes from behind me, catching me off guard. I hadn't noticed him behind the counter, gripping it tightly as his gaze pierces the parking lot.

I quickly turn away from him. The last thing I need is a final vision of the way the late-afternoon light captures Randy's insanely perfect face haunting me throughout dinner with Jeremy.

"And you look first date perfect," Sarah says from behind the counter.

"I agree," Rita chimes in. "Not a lot of skin but still very sexy. You nailed it."

For some reason, I can feel Randy cringing at their compliments as I manage a weak "Thank you both" while continuing to scan the parking lot for the red Mercedes-Benz I damaged. "Where is he?" I mutter, checking my watch.

"He's here," Randy says, his voice cutting through my anxiety. "He's in the black Maserati. His car is in the shop, getting fixed."

I deliberately continue to avoid looking at Randy. But soon, the energy emanating from his body is wedged against my backside. He's standing right behind me.

"See?" His deep voice slips against my ear. His extended arm huddles near my shoulder as he points at Jeremy's car.

My heart skips a beat. What he's doing is not fair, and he knows it. I hurriedly spot Jeremy emerging from the Maserati and making his way toward us.

This is the last thing I need—an awkward encounter between my date and my… Randy. Sarah and Rita are already gushing about how handsome Jeremy looks, saying he is dressed to the nines, as I step outside the café.

The cool early evening air not only stops Jeremy in his tracks, but it also brings me a sigh of relief, washing away the uneasy thrill that being near Randy had stirred in me.

"Hey," I say to Jeremy, finally standing directly in front of him. He smells great, and my coworkers weren't exaggerating; he looks incredibly handsome in a camel-colored duster coat, dark dress pants, and a cream cable-knit sweater. Clearly, Jeremy knows how to choose his outfits to complement his attributes.

"A Maserati?" I can't help but ask. My curiosity is piqued by the vehicle's sheer ostentatiousness.

"Just for the night. Just for you," he responds smoothly. His breath carries a fresh hint of spearmint.

Looking up into his eyes, I find them twinkling with flirtation. Any girl would be thrilled to spend an evening with a man like him, yet my mind keeps wanting to grab memories of intense moments with Randy.

I wonder if it's too late to ask Jeremy to simply hand me the bill for his car's repairs; though judging by his choice of transport, he hardly needs my financial contribution. It's clear that Jeremy is the type of man you consider when you're ready to settle down with a serious partner. I mean, look at him. He's nice. He has money. He smells delicious. But am I really ready to get serious? The thought flickers through my mind, daring me to say yes. Perhaps I could be. I should at least give it a try.

With this newfound resolve, I don't retreat from the date. Instead, I find myself curious about the night ahead. "So where are you taking me tonight?" I ask, open to the possibilities this evening with Jeremy might unveil.

WE'RE HEADING DOWNTOWN TO THE BLUE TAVERN, a spot I'm familiar with. It's an American bistro with a menu that's never disappointed me. Jeremy has made an impressive choice—it says he knows his way around good food.

Riding in the Maserati feels like being in a piece of art—too pristine and luxurious for a casual drive on a chilly New England evening. I'm almost afraid to touch anything, feeling out of place in such a meticulously maintained environment. It feels more like a museum exhibit than a car, something to be admired rather than used. Jeremy, on the other hand, seems perfectly at ease, engaging me in conversation as he endeavors to learn more about me.

My responses to his questions have been fairly standard. Yes, I'm an only child. Yes, I've grown up in this charming midsize town. No, I'm not opposed to the idea of moving away someday. My parents are still together, and honestly, I couldn't ask for better ones than Faye and Harold.

But then Jeremy asks, "Do you want to start a family of your own one day?" It's a question that makes me pause, requiring me to ponder not just my immediate future, but what I truly desire in the long run.

As I attempt to picture myself in a wedding gown, my imagination drifts to extravagant settings and idyllic scenes of a dome ceiling adorned with flowers. Then I imagine a beach with waves caressing the shore, me walking barefoot along-side… My thoughts are interrupted when I catch a glimpse of Jeremy. His face is a mix of amusement and curiosity, clearly intrigued by my hesitation.

And now my thoughts have gone blank. "Why? Are you looking for a wife?" I find myself asking, deciding to shift the direction of our conversation to something that takes me out of the hot seat. It seems like the best way to navigate this moment is to start asking my own questions.

Jeremy's response comes with a chuckle, as if my sudden interrogation amuses him. "No, just making conversation," he assures me.

My eyes wander around the car's luxurious interior—the soft leather, the polished wood paneling.

"Well, you definitely can afford one if you are," I remark, half-joking, half-serious.

Jeremy's laughter fills the car again. "You're funny, Gina. And you have great timing."

Emboldened, perhaps, by his easy demeanor, I venture into more sensitive territory. "What about Randy?" I begin, curiosity getting the better of me. I've been itching to dig a little deeper into the background of my enigmatic boss. Steve, the café owner, who's also another one of Randy's cousins, could have been a source, but he's hardly the type to chitchat. Nobody is more intense than Steve. Half the time, I'm not sure he knows if he's coming or going.

At the mention of Randy, however, I sense a shift in Jeremy's mood.

"What about him?" he asks, his voice suddenly tight.

I press on, hoping to peel back some of the layers of mystery surrounding Randy. "Where's he from?"

Jeremy pauses, rubbing his face thoughtfully as if my question requires significant contemplation.

I'm surprised by his hesitation. "Is that such a hard question to answer?"

"No, no…" Jeremy finally responds with a slight

edge of reluctance still in his voice. “He grew up here, like you.”

“Really?” I’m genuinely taken aback. “I never heard of him before I started working for him.” Considering Randy is only four years older than I am, I would’ve thought someone as gorgeous and charismatic as him would have left a mark on Roosevelt High School’s collective memory. Or maybe he went to Mid-City High School. Naomi attended that high school, though. She would have undoubtedly heard about him if he’d gone there. However, she hadn’t heard of him before he started at the Calypso either.

Jeremy shifts uncomfortably, picking up on my astonishment. “He’s your boss, right?”

“Yes,” I respond, my tone far from enthusiastic. “I know he’s your cousin and all, but he can be such an asshole.”

My blunt assessment earns another chuckle from Jeremy.

I tilt my head curiously. “You don’t agree?”

“No. I don’t agree,” he answers convincingly, still wearing a grin.

His disagreement irks me, yet for some reason, I find myself believing him. I purse my lips, sifting through my memories for instances where Randy was particularly harsh with me. But then I start to wonder how he interacts with Sarah, Rita, and Pete? Or any of the other employees, for that matter? In the midst of our own tumultuous interactions, I've neglected to notice how he consistently behaves with others.

"So, why do you say my cousin's an asshole?" Jeremy's question feels like a match to my fuse of pent-up frustrations.

"Where do I start? The beginning, middle, the end?" I retort, feeling a mix of anger and relief at the opportunity to unload.

Jeremy's eyebrows rise in surprise as he keeps his focus on the road. "Wow. That bad, huh?"

I nod vigorously, primed to spill every detail about Randy's behavior—a side of him that Jeremy seems oblivious to. And with that, I dive into my story, starting from the very beginning, laying out the sequence of events that led me to form such a strong opinion about his not-so-perfect cousin.

As we walk together through the quaint cobblestone courtyard toward the restaurant, I'm aware of how much I've been talking. It's a lot, even for me, but Jeremy did ask why his cousin is such a jerk, and somehow, I feel like I've barely scratched the surface in making my case against Randy. My mind is still racing with scenarios as the hostess leads us to our table, which is a bit of a shame because I usually revel in the ambiance of Blue Tavern the moment I step inside.

The restaurant always welcomes patrons with its charming atmosphere. Rustic tables are topped with candles nestled in glass orbs that resemble snowballs. They cast a soft glow throughout the enchanting space. The warmth is tangible, not just from the candlelight alone but also from walls painted in an antique blue mixed with delicate gold flecks that catch the light and cast a rich, inviting glow throughout the dining room. It's an effect I would usually take a moment to appreciate fully. However, tonight, my focus is elsewhere. Seated now, with our drink orders placed and menus in hand, I feel an urgent need to continue my story. It seems important that Jeremy understands this side of Randy.

"Did you know he actually tried to lecture me on the 'right' way to clean a table? Talk about harassment," I continue, my frustration laid bare. "And the irony? He leaves the kitchen counters a disaster after he's done cooking. We're always cleaning up after Mr. Big-Time Manhattan Chef. I mean, I get that he's a celebrity chef, but there's a limit, right?" I place my menu down, aiming to catch Jeremy's full attention, which seems partly caught by his own menu.

"Right," he says as if he's placating me. Then he asks, "Do you know what you want to order?"

Cold air douses my eyes as they grow wide. I really need him to listen and grasp the entirety of my experience with Randy. It's important that he understands my perspective is rooted in genuine evidence. "I'm having the maple-glazed salmon."

Jeremy's attention is still glued to his menu, which makes me want to rein in my rant about Randy. Yet I find myself unable to stop, even as a sliver of reason suggests I should.

"So, Gina, do you have a boyfriend?" he asks, his eyes still buried in his menu. *Well, that was a curveball he just threw.*

"Of course I don't have a boyfriend," I reply, a bit bewildered. "I wouldn't be here with you if I did."

Finally, I said something that made him look up from his menu. His eyes meet mine with a spark. "Oh, then I have a chance?"

What he just asked kind of registers, but it kind of doesn't either. I'm not ready to shift gears just yet. "Can I just finish this story?" I insist. It's still important to me that Jeremy understands my viewpoint on Randy, especially since he doesn't seem fully convinced yet.

Acknowledging my persistence, Jeremy finally sets his menu aside to give me his full attention. "Which story?" he asks.

I think he's a little annoyed, but I don't care. He must understand how I arrived at my viewpoint about Randy. So I revisit the story about how Randy critiqued my table-cleaning skills, suggesting absurdly that my method could lead to the restaurant being shut down because I was spreading bacteria.

"That's not even a thing," I say, throwing my hands up in exasperation.

Okay, so I'm all worked up now and shaking my head as another memory about Randy comes to mind, one way worse than the table thing, and I must share it.

CHAPTER 4

Off Limits

GINA

WAKING UP THIS FRIDAY, I'm relieved the week is nearly over, but I'm also troubled by a nagging regret. I realize I wasn't the best company for Jeremy during last night's first date. I couldn't seem to steer the conversation away from Randy, and now I'm worried I might have overshared. Jeremy was so quiet on the way home that I'm left doubting if there'll be a second date, let alone a third.

And then there was that moment he asked if he had a chance with me. He was so sincere. Truthfully, I don't know the answer. It's not that I'm not interested; it's just that I've always struggled with making clear choices.

Take my college years, for instance. I spent four years working toward a biology degree, fighting through every test, paper, and lab. Finishing with a 2.7 GPA, the dream of becoming a doctor—of making a meaningful difference in people's lives—faded when my academic advisor suggested delaying graduation to retake courses and improve my GPA. *Sigh...*

Just like that, the reality hit me. Was I really cut out for a life spent diagnosing and treating others? At age twenty-one, despite four years of college, I found myself more uncertain about my future than ever.

Helping Naomi study for the LSAT and then taking the test alongside her as a gesture of support brought an unexpected twist. Once again, I was on my way down what I thought would be another solid career path. I scored 160, a surprise to both of us given Naomi's impressive 176. Yet, it didn't take long, only about a year, for me to realize that the law wasn't for me either. Still, I went through the motions, even attempting the bar exam three times. Each time I stared down at that test, my mind went blank. Plus, the idea of standing in a courtroom and debating legalities felt utterly foreign to me. I was indifferent to winning or losing legal battles?

But when it comes to food? That's where my heart truly lies. Culinary school was a true revelation. It's where I earn consistent A's and praise from chef instructors. I really like cooking. I like learning all the techniques and pairings when it comes to seasonings. I relish studying the secrets behind making food taste exceptionally flavorful and cooking my meats until they're as tender as butter. And the sauces—oh, I've learned to make my sauces so delicious, they'll melt in any taster's mouth. Yes, I love all of that. But baking and making desserts and pastries bring me the most joy.

There is an indescribable satisfaction in watching others relish the various breads and sweet creations that I whip up. The look of pure satisfaction on their faces brings me abundant joy, a sense of accomplishment that feels like it has meaning. This is where my future is meant to unfold—in the kitchen, not in a courtroom. Yet when it comes to relationships, clarity still seems to elude me.

Today, I'm back at work. And Randy, with his knack for complicating my feelings, has been distant for most of my shift, only to suddenly appear, all wired up and asking me to join him at the back counter to show me something.

"You see this number?" he asks. I instantly recognize the rhetorical tone in his voice, a familiar prelude to one of his 'teachable moments.' "We have to account for every grain of flour that's used." His lecture begins as if today were my first day on the job.

I can't help but roll my eyes, my default response. I wish Jeremy could witness this perfect example of the behavior I spent so much of our date trying to explain. If he were a witness to this, then he would understand why I couldn't stop going on and on about his cousin.

Standing my ground, arms folded and adrenaline surging through me, I'm ready for whatever confrontation comes next. "What's that got to do with me?" I manage to politely ask, barely masking my aggravation.

"You didn't ask if you could make your lemon pastries this week." That patronizing smirk of his makes me want to… *Ugh.*

But I hold my composure. "What lemon pastries?" I feign ignorance, though I'm fully aware what he's referring to. If Randy insists on picking this battle, then he'd better get his facts straight.

His expression twists in silent accusation. He knows that I know exactly which pastries he's referring to. "There's a budget, Gina, and if you're going to keep this going, then I have to make sure we can pay for it."

As Randy's intense gaze meets mine, I can't help but notice, despite everything, how striking his eyes are. Still, I am not deterred. "Are you kidding me?" I challenge him, rendered incredulous by his audacity.

"No," he replies, dead serious.

Taking a moment, I look carefully at the pastry counter before proceeding. Then I watch Randy's eyes, giving him one last chance to save himself. Of course, he doesn't take it. "You should be kidding me," I declare. "Because as you can clearly see by the empty pastry container, we are now sold out of my… what?"

"Sold out of your what?" he echoes, sounding confused about what I'm asking.

I relish that puzzled look on his face. "You said they were lemon pastries, but they were not. They were raspberry vanilla swirl cro-muffins. So if you're complaining about the flour used for lemon pastries because those items aren't selling, then you're barking up the wrong tree because *my* baked goods have sold out."

Good, he hasn't dropped my favorite expression of his. Well, my third favorite expression of his. My first is when we're in the throes of passion and Randy looks blissfully satisfied. I am just that satisfied right now, having wiped that smug look off his face. Sometimes when I'm arguing with Randy, all those law school classes definitely come in handy.

Just as Randy gears up for his rebuttal, a voice calls out. This is a voice that tugs at my heartstrings and cuts through the tension. "Oh, Gina?"

"Mom?" I respond even before my eyes find her. This is a surprise that sends a wave of warmth through me considering it has been two weeks since I last saw her. That's a rarity since my parents live only ten minutes from my apartment. They also have a washer and dryer that I use to do my laundry, which is currently overflowing in my laundry basket. I've just been so busy lately.

I hurry over, and we exchange kisses across the counter.

"What are you doing here?" I ask.

"I happened to be in the neighborhood, and it's been ages since I've seen you," she explains with a gentle pinch to my chin. "Plus, I've been dying to taste those raspberry vanilla swirl cro-muffins everyone's been raving about."

Before I can even turn to flash Randy a self-satisfied grin, one that silently conveys, "See? My mom remembers the pastries I make, and she's not even profiting from them," I realize he's already standing beside me with his arm outstretched. Surprised, I twist slightly to face him, my expression inquisitive.

"Hello, I'm Randy," he croons.

Catching the charm he's throwing, my mom's eyes light up as they shift between Randy and me, silently urging me to exhibit the manners she instilled in me.

"Right," I mumble. Suddenly, my face flushes with warmth, and my head begins to spin. Strangely, my legs feel weak, as if I might actually faint if I don't compose myself. Gathering my thoughts, I manage to introduce them, albeit somewhat clumsily. "Randy, this is my mother, Faye. Faye, I mean, Mom, this is Randy."

"It's a pleasure to finally meet you, Faye," Randy says, his tone syrupier than before. The agitation and snarkiness I faced earlier have completely melted away from him and have been replaced by a warm smile directed at my mom—an inviting gesture not even reserved for our regular customers.

"I know who you are. It's nice to meet you too," Mom responds, as if she has already been briefed about Randy, which I'm certain I haven't done.

"Mom, I've never mentioned Randy to you," I interject quickly, just in case he gets the wrong idea.

My mom gives me a curious frown. "I know, but his food is the talk of the town."

"I know, but I don't… Just…" My eyes squeeze shut as I fish for the right words, not wanting Randy to think I've been discussing him with my family as if he's more than just a casual fling.

"Are you feeling all right, honey?" My mom appears slightly concerned but more amused. "Did you have shellfish for lunch?" She then turns her attention to Randy. "Gina tends to get anxious when she eats shellfish. It's the mercury."

Mom, please, I plead silently, hoping we can cease discussing personal matters with Randy.

"I don't think she had shellfish today," Randy interjects smoothly. *Oh, that grin. I could just eat him alive.* "Maybe last night. She went on a date with my cousin, Jeremy. He's a nice guy, just so you know."

My horror deepens at Randy's disclosure.

"A date? Well, that's nice," my mom responds passively. "How about having dinner with us on Saturday night?" she asks, getting to the crux of her surprise visit. "Then you can tell Dad and me all about your date with this handsome man's cousin."

She winks mischievously. "Unless you've got other plans, of course."

"No, I don't have other plans," I murmur, hanging my head, my face burning with embarrassment.

"Good, because we just want to see that lovely face of the daughter we made. Hear her voice..." My mom inhales deeply through her nose. "Smell her skin," she says dramatically.

Randy chuckles, evidently amused by my mom's quirky sense of humor.

She's grinning from ear to ear. My mom loves it when someone appreciates her unique brand of wit.

Before I can break the two up, Brady, one of the kitchen staff, thankfully interrupts by poking his head into the front of the café to inform Randy that everything is prepped for the dinner crowd.

"Right. Be right there," Randy responds before turning his attention back to my mom. "Are you staying for dinner, Faye?"

"No," my mom and I answer simultaneously.

Startled by our chorus, Mom shoots me a perplexed frown, as if questioning my sanity.

"I mean, I'm assuming you're not staying because Dad isn't with you," I quickly add.

"No, he's not," Mom whispers, her gaze

piercing through me. I can tell she senses something off about my behavior.

Randy smoothly assures my mom that it was a pleasure to meet her and generously offers that anything she orders tonight will be on the house. Then he pivots to me. "Gina, we're short-staffed tonight. Could you cover some tables until your shift ends?"

My mouth drops open, totally caught off guard. Randy knows I'm supposed to start working with Pete in about an hour. I won't argue with him in front of my mom, and he seems to be well aware of that.

"Sure thing, boss," I manage to say, though my eyes shoot daggers at him.

He chuckles—a deep, taunting sound—as he heads to the kitchen.

What an ass. Score one for him.

Oddly enough, I'm still fuming hours after my mom's departure, even though when she left, I promised to eat dinner with them on Saturday night, which usually makes me happy. I'm one of those people who loves hanging out with their parents. But I'm angry because Randy was charming, almost in a scheming way. It feels like he ultimately used the interaction with my mom to get me to stand down, and that doesn't sit right with me.

I would be angrier if I hadn't gotten so much exercise by moving from table to table, but the nonstop hustle quelled my irritation. The evening rush kept us exceptionally busy. Even though we don't officially have wait staff, the combination of Randy's culinary expertise and our warm service consistently encourages diners to leave generous tips. Now, as the shift winds down, Sarah and I find a moment to take our final break together.

Tonight's "Star Chef Special"—Randy's brown butter lamb ravioli—was a massive hit with customers. I've been on my feet for three hours straight, receiving all kinds of "compliments to the chef" that I'll never deliver.

"Mmm." Sarah's eyes roll back in delight as she takes a bite of the ravioli. "This man definitely knows how to cook."

Reluctantly, I have to admit that she's right. Randy's culinary skills are undeniably impressive. However, this seems like the perfect moment to ask Sarah something that has been on my mind since last night.

"So, Sarah—" I take a bite of ravioli. "What's it like working for Randy? Do you find him as annoying as I do?"

"Oh, you two," she says with a laugh. "I find him friendly, Gina. He's been a game-changer for Calypso Café. He's like a big fish in a small pond, and he seems content with that, which is great. Well, thanks to you."

"Thanks to me?" I blurt out, taken aback.

"He loves bantering with you," Sarah says matter-of-factly, as if it's common knowledge. "You both thrive on it. And by the way, you're not fooling anybody. The way you two look at each other. All chemistry and sexual tension." She shrugs, her eyebrows animatedly raised.

I'm so shocked by her words that I feel utterly exposed, as if I've been left out in the cold, bare and vulnerable.

"I don't have feelings for him in any way." Even though I'm strongly protesting, my insides feel as if I'm making a feeble attempt at convincing her.

Sarah serves herself another hearty helping of ravioli, while I find myself silently appreciative that Randy left enough on the plate for both of us. We're famished, and it shows in the way we're eating. "Is that so?" she asks, sounding far too nonchalant for my liking.

"Yes! Absolutely."

Sarah just shrugs. "Okay, then."

Her indifference irks me. I feel like she's not taking me seriously. "I really don't!" I insist.

"Whatever, Gina."

This whole verbal exchange feels like a train-wreck. Just because there's a physical attraction and some chemistry between us doesn't mean I actually like him. And clearly, he doesn't like me in that way either. Sarah calls what he does "banter"? That sounds like a sugarcoated way of excusing his behavior. All these thoughts are swirling around, ready to burst out, when my Apple Watch beeps. Relieved for the distraction, I eagerly answer it, grateful for the chance to divert my thoughts from this mess.

"Hi, Gina. It's Jeremy." His voice cuts through the crisp late-afternoon air.

Sarah's eyes are fixed on my lips, as though she's hanging on every word I'm about to say. I wish I had my AirPods to make this a bit more private, but they're in my purse, which is in my locker.

"Hi, Jeremy," I manage, forcing a smile that

feels genuine. But if being honest, I'm surprised to hear from him.

"I was wondering, do you have any plans for tonight?" he asks.

I hesitate, keenly aware of Sarah's intense gaze fixed on me as if she's determined to catch every nuance of my response. "Um, no. I guess not," I say, a bit unnerved by her scrutiny.

"How about dinner?" Jeremy proposes.

Glancing at the large plate of food on the table, mostly devoured by Sarah, I reply, "Sure."

Sarah silently claps and mouths, "Good answer."

Jeremy adds, "Oh, and how about we keep talk of Randy off the table tonight? I'd rather know more about you."

In a moment of panic, I quickly agree, telling him he can pick me up at The Calypso at 7 p.m., before ending the call swiftly. I avoided making eye contact with Sarah during the last part of my conversation with Jeremy. But now, facing the music, I look at her. Sarah's eyebrows are raised in a "told-you-so" manner, as if to say, "See? I was right about you and Randy, wasn't I?"

CHAPTER 5
Where to Run?
GINA

FOUR HOURS LATER

THE DATE WAS UNEXPECTEDLY FANTASTIC. Jeremy's curiosity about the choices I've made in life led to a deep conversation. As I recounted my decisions, I felt a bit erratic in my life's direction. Yet if Jeremy shared that impression, he concealed it masterfully.

The subject of Randy didn't come up, allowing me to learn more about Jeremy too. He resides in what I would describe as a luxury apartment in Boston, a detail he downplayed, and why he's here in a humble town is still cloaked in privacy. In his professional life, though, he's a financier for insurance companies. He also opened up about more personal matters, revealing he is divorced and has a son named Jude, who is ten. Jude has a passion for science and math, and though he splits his time between both parents, he spends every weekend with Jeremy in Boston.

As we walk along the pier, the gentle stroll helps us digest our delightful dinner. While the meal was enjoyable, I can't help but think it still falls short of Randy's ravioli. But that's as much as I'll dwell on Randy for now. True, my last thought of him was a fond one, yet typically, my thoughts about him skew toward the negative. And tonight is too splendid for such negativity. The air is refreshingly brisk, and the moon casts a mesmerizing reflection on the bay, creating a perfect, tranquil atmosphere.

Sparked by lingering curiosity, I venture to ask, "Then you've been in love?"

"I suppose so," Jeremy responds, looking up with a contemplative expression. "The thing is, I still love her," he discloses.

My intrigued "Hmm" encourages him to share more. Jeremy opens up about his ex-wife, April, revealing they were college sweethearts who tied the knot right after high school. As time passed, they gradually acknowledged they were evolving in different directions, a turn of events not uncommon for young lovers. This realization led to an amicable separation. These days, Jeremy and April share a bond that's more familial than romantic, particularly since April has remarried. Her new husband, Eddie, comes highly recommended by Jeremy, who praises him not only as a fantastic stepfather to his son but also as a genuinely good person.

Wearing his trademark flirtatious smile, Jeremy playfully remarks, "April made a good choice, which means I've got to step up my game too."

I can't help but snort sarcastically, asking, "Then why are you out with me?"

His laughter is infectious, and his smile deepens, becoming even more enticing. "Because you're beautiful," he asserts.

My heart races as I lower my gaze, trying to process this overwhelming sensation stirring within me. "But so was Cinderella's evil stepmother. The point being that you should not pick a stepmother for your son based on looks alone."

Then, in a moment that feels both bold and gentle, Jeremy reaches for my hand and holds it in his. "That's exactly why we're here—to get to know each other better and find out if we click."

I do my best to maintain a steady smile as I look

into Jeremy's radiant expression. It's clear that he's genuinely into me. Yet I can't shake the thought that Randy and I have never actually been on a proper date—a glaring sign that he doesn't see a future with me. Plus, it's a big reason why there's so much about him I don't know. Like the story behind the tattoo on Randy's forearm, which I've always been curious about. Jeremy might know, and as much as I would like to ask him, I can't, having promised to steer clear of the topic of Randy.

"Tell me more about yourself," Jeremy requests, pulling me back from my thoughts.

I hesitate, feeling like I've already shared the highlights of my life. "Like what?"

"When was the last time you went on a date?"

The answer comes more easily than I expect. "Well, yesterday," I coyly admit.

Jeremy's laughter is warm. "You enjoy making jokes, huh? It's cute."

I find myself looking down, focusing on the wooden planks of the pier, watching the dark water glint through the narrow gaps. The realization that he took my statement as a joke—and that I didn't even recognize it as such until he laughed—hits me. I've been dodging the real answer, but suddenly, I'm overwhelmed by the urge to be honest. He deserves to know the truth. After all, I'm becoming increasingly entangled in this complicated situation with his cousin, who seems to have a phobia of commitment.

"I haven't been on a proper date in ages," I finally confess, lifting my head, prepared to divulge the reasons behind my statement. But as the words are about to tumble out, my gaze lands on a figure in the distance. The way he moves, the posture, his hands buried in the pockets of his peacoat—a coat I've become all too familiar with—it's unmistakably Randy. This is the first time I've ever bumped into him outside in the wild.

"Gina?" Jeremy's voice, tinged with worry, breaks through my shock.

I'm frozen in place, my heart sinking to my feet, as Jeremy strides a few steps ahead, unaware of the person who has seized my attention. My gaze remains locked on Randy—the man who is essentially my only romantic partner.

And he's not alone. He is accompanied by a woman whose features are too distant to fully appreciate, yet it's clear that she's striking. They seem comfortable with each other, unmistakably on a date, and his date isn't me. The realization stings, prompting tears to gather in my eyes, an emotional response I desperately wish to suppress. Why should this sight cause me such pain?

Feeling a sharp twist in my stomach, I manage to say, "Sorry. I'm not feeling well." That's the understatement of the year. My stomach churns unpleasantly, and I'm acutely aware that continuing in this direction means an unavoidable encounter with the couple—an encounter for which I am utterly unprepared, emotionally or otherwise.

"Okay, well, I'll drive you home," Jeremy offers.

I quickly raise my hand, signaling him to stop. "No." I take steps backward, creating more space between Jeremy and myself, though it still doesn't feel like enough.

"Sure, I'll drive you," he persists.

I shake my head frantically, turning away from him and increasing my pace to almost a run. Trying to keep my voice low enough to evade Randy's ears, I call out, "Don't follow me. Just… I need to go."

"Gina!" he calls after me, but I wish he wouldn't say my name.

I'm not turning back. My legs seem to move of their own accord, propelling me forward as I start to run. I wipe away tears that insist on revealing my emotions. I don't want to feel this hurt, but I do. At this moment, fleeing feels like my only option, even if it makes me feel like a coward.

Drenched in sweat, I dash up the dock, passing by storefronts and restaurants. To escape the gaze of curious onlookers, I veer into the nearest tree-lined residential street, pushing my body harder than I have in a long time. I feel utterly lost until I call Naomi, confessing that I ran away from my date.

"Can you pick me up?" I ask desperately.

"I'll be right there," she said without hesitation. "Where are you?"

I send her my location and wait, feeling utterly embarrassed. Reflecting on what just happened, I regret not facing Randy and his date directly. I can't believe I mishandled the situation so badly.

As I pace back and forth on the sidewalk in front of a perfectly manicured lawn, I replay a different version of the encounter in my mind.

"Your date looks lovely, Randy," I would start, paying homage to Barbara Streisand in 'The Way We Were.' I imagine his puzzled expression as he tries to decipher my angle. Eventually, he'd manage a polite, "Thank you."

Then, with a bit of mystery, I would drop a

hint, saying, "This little meeting of ours is bound to change things, don't you think?"

His date and Jeremy would be clueless, but Randy would understand the underlying message—that things between us have to change.

I'M STILL SHIVERING, SOMETHING I DIDN'T NOTICE until Naomi arrives in her silk pajamas. She had been watching a movie on Netflix with her fiancé, Derek, when I called. Without a second thought, she slipped into her tennis shoes, donned a coat, and came to my rescue. Now, in the warmth of Naomi's new car—its heater warding off the cold, its ride smooth, quiet, and comfortable—I realize my shivering is less about being chilly and more about the adrenaline settling in my body.

"What happened?" Naomi asks, her concern evident. That was her second question; her first had been whether I was hurt. To which I answered, "Only my pride."

I recount to Naomi the events leading up to my abrupt exit, specifically viewing Randy with his date. I don't confess the extent of the pain that sight caused me, seeing him with another woman—even though Naomi is the person I confide in about everything.

"Jeez, Gina," Naomi responds, her sigh heavy with a mix of concern and fatigue. "So what's your plan?"

"What do you mean?" I snap back, a defensive edge creeping into my voice. Being friends with Naomi for so long, I can almost anticipate where her questions are leading. I brace myself, trying to think of something to say that might steer the conversation away from areas I'm not ready to delve into. "I mean, there's nothing I can do. I'm just the girl Randy screws, and she's the one he takes out on a date."

Naomi, unfazed by my tone of defeat, simply signals a turn with the car's blinker. "There's always something you can do, Gina. Every action we take is a choice. Now that you know more, you have the opportunity to make a different choice."

"Oh, goodness," I moan, rolling my eyes and slouching deeper into the leather seats, wishing I could just melt away. "Don't make this into a courtroom drama or therapy session, Nom. Fine, yes, I've got more insight now. Sure, I can stop sleeping with him."

"But that's only if you don't actually have feelings for him," she interjects promptly. "If you're bolting because he's with someone else, then…" She trails off, letting a simple shrug convey the rest of her thought.

I turn away, facing the passenger door, showing Naomi my back as I rest my head against the seat. "I know," I murmur as fresh tears start to fill my eyes. "I know what I have to do."

CHAPTER 6

Dining and Dodging with Parents

GINA

I ASKED Naomi to take me directly home last night instead of taking me back to the café to pick up my car—a decision I'm now thankful for. This morning, I received a voicemail from Jeremy detailing how he waited for me before eventually coming to the conclusion that I wouldn't return. Despite his repeated phone calls, which I didn't answer, and his voicemails requesting callbacks to discuss things properly, I find myself unable to reach out to him. I'm still unsure of what to say.

Before bed, I was primed to confront him with the truth, but after a night of restless sleep, my resolve has faded, now overshadowed by a sense of embarrassment. Jeremy, with his keen perception, will likely connect the dots and conclude that my sudden departure was tied to some unresolved feelings I might have for his cousin—a notion that Naomi subtly suggested last night, even if she didn't say it outright. Thankfully, I'm off work today. The Calypso doesn't serve dinner on Sunday evenings, and for that reason, Randy usually takes that day off. Basically, there's no risk of an awkward encounter between us until Monday. It's then that I'll have to be straightforward with him: us having sex must end. And with that, a chapter closes.

So this morning, before Calypso opened, I caught an Uber to pick up my car simply to avoid seeing anyone at all. Since returning home, I've thrown myself into a flurry of activities to keep my mind off things. My routine cleaning of the apartment, a task reserved for my Saturdays off, was where I started. Following that, I dove into baking, creating a large batch of raspberry vanilla swirl cream cro-muffins. I carefully placed these divine pastries into a large pink box, one that could comfortably fit two dozen treats. With the box of desserts and a hefty load of laundry in tow, I then made my way to my parents' house.

Mom and Dad bought this enchanting Tudor-style house, constructed in 1902, when I was just six years old. They initially described it as a "fixer-upper," yet it wasn't until I reached the age of ten that it truly transformed into the dream home they had always imagined. I adore this house. Crossing its threshold instantly eases me; my mind halts its relentless strategizing of how to maintain distance from Randy, especially since I suspect he and Jeremy might have finally run into each other on the pier. I've even imagined their possible exchange:

"Hey, Jeremy. What brings you here?" Randy might have asked.

"I was on a date with Gina, but I think she bolted when she saw you. One minute she was right beside me, and the next, she's running away," the Jeremy in my mind replied, searching longingly behind him for any sign of me. Then he turned to Randy and asked, "Any idea what might have prompted that?"

In the comforting embrace of my childhood home, I find relief from dwelling on last night's embarrassment. Since arriving, I've kept busy—preparing dough for bread to go with dinner, which will be my mom's signature beef stroganoff, my favorite. She also asked me to sort through my bedroom for items to donate to charity. Although I live on my own now, that room still holds a special place as mine in what my parents affectionately call our "forever home," free for me to use as I see fit. And of course, I've been washing, drying, and folding a mountain of laundry.

"Gina, dinner's ready!" My mom's voice carries into the laundry room from downstairs.

"On my way!" I call back, tossing my final load of damp clothes into the dryer.

Just as I'm about to head to the kitchen table, I grab my cell phone off the top of the washing machine. It immediately begins to ring. It's Jeremy calling again. I hesitate, uncertain about answering. By the third ring, his call goes to voicemail.

Why didn't I just answer? It's not like me to shy away from hard conversations. This whole situation only stiffens my resolve to do whatever it takes to end the sex-only relationship between Randy and me.

Next, I elevate my avoidance tactics by intentionally leaving my cell phone on the washing machine. This way, if Jeremy calls again, I won't have to handle it in front of my parents. They typically don't pry into my personal life, but they are astute at reading my reactions. They would instantly sense something was amiss if they saw how I reacted to Jeremy's name popping up on my screen. That's precisely why I choose to leave it in the laundry room—so that won't happen.

ALL DAY LONG, MY DAD HAS BEEN ISOLATED IN THE backyard casita, busy working on a mysterious project. In our household, we stick to an unspoken rule: we refrain from probing about our individual endeavors until we're gathered around the dinner table.

Savoring the beef stroganoff, its flavors dissolving deliciously in my mouth, I pause before helping myself to another generous bite. Dinner has officially begun, so I'm able to finally turn to my father and ask, "Okay, Dad, what have you been working on in the backyard?"

My parents exchange a meaningful glance, and I immediately try to decipher it. My mom's eyes sparkle with excitement, while a subtle smile plays on my dad's lips. They're at it again. I recognize the looks on their faces. They're up to something exciting, innovative, or what some might deem unconventional.

My mom sits up straighter, exuding confidence.

"Love Bug, you're now looking at one of the cohosts of the *Empty Nesters Who Lunch* podcast."

"Faye's diving back into her comedic roots," my dad says.

"We'll be airing our shows Monday through Friday from noon to one, and we'll also broadcast live on YouTube. We're doing big things," my mom adds, exchanging a wink with my dad. "And Harold here is the producer and director." Harold, of course, is my dad.

I freeze midbite. "Wow. That's quite the shift from dentistry, isn't it, Dad?"

Sitting his fork in his bowl to proudly cross his arms, Dad announces, "I've retired."

"Oh," I manage to say as childhood memories float through my mind. As a kid, I spent so much time after school in my dad's front office, doing homework while waiting for my mom, who worked at the municipal library, to pick me up.

"Yes. From dentist to director, Love Bug," he declares, smiling as he dabs the corners of his mouth with his white napkin.

"Well, congratulations, Dad," I offer before I continue scarfing down the best comfort food on the planet.

My mom watches me with an inquisitive gaze. "What's going on with you?" she asks.

I halt, my fork halfway to my mouth. "What do you mean?" I reply, trying to sound as nonchalant as possible.

"You're eating very quickly. Plus, you've been somewhat distant since you got here. So, what's bothering you, Love Bug?"

"Nothing," I assert, even though my voice betrays me with a slight crack. Deep down, I'm yearning to break down in my mom's embrace and confess the entire debacle of last night. It would sure be nice to tell her about my decision to end things with Randy, one that's tearing me apart. She always knows what to say to make me feel better. But I can't tell her what's wrong with me. I've never engaged in a relationship like the one I'm in with Randy. Casual sex is not my style.

My parents know me to be someone who holds off being intimate in a relationship until I'm sure there's reciprocation. The mere acknowledgment that my libido and not my brain has been driving my relationship with Randy feels so wrong, especially against the backdrop of my parents' thirty-year testament to love and companionship. They are not just spouses but best friends, always there to support one another through thick and thin.

Growing up, I would come home to find them at the kitchen table, working through whatever challenges they faced with open communication and understanding. And here I am, entangled with a man I can't stand, trapped in a cycle of frustrating conversations and interactions coupled with fleeting but highly enjoyable passionate encounters. Randy is stubborn and never admits fault. Sure, there are moments when his better qualities peek through, but those are too often eclipsed by his insufferable behavior.

"Oh, it's definitely something," my dad interjects, his intuition clearly catching the nuances in my voice.

I'm so on the spot that I can feel my shoulder blades begin to pinch.

"Is it Randy, the one who introduced himself to me yesterday?" my mom asks.

The fact that my dad doesn't ask, "Who's Randy?" and instead waits for my response clues me in that they've already had a conversation about him. That's how well we all know each other. It has only been the three of us, all of our lives, living, learning, and loving one another. We have all gotten pretty good at picking up on things.

"No," I respond, my voice pitching higher in a less-than-convincing attempt to deny it.

"He was really smitten by her, Harold."

"I heard," my dad says.

I'm shaking my head vigorously, eager to correct their misunderstanding. "He's not smitten by me, Mom. Actually, it's the complete opposite. Right before you came in yesterday, he was lecturing me about using too much flour. So, no—definitely not smitten." Also, there's the fact that last night he was on a date with another woman, but I wouldn't dare mention that to them.

"Using too much flour?" My dad sounds genuinely baffled by the concept.

"Yes, according to him, I apparently use too much flour when I make my cro-muffins, which he'd prefer I didn't do for some odd reason." I lift a finger, suddenly experiencing a lightbulb moment. "Ah, now I get it. It's because he doesn't want me to succeed," I say, my tone reaching a dramatic crescendo.

My parents give me a look that suggests they think I might be spiraling a bit. Admittedly, discussions about Randy have a unique way of getting under my skin. Not wanting them to see me like this, I plaster on an exaggerated smile, which only prompts my dad to arch an eyebrow in response.

Great. Now I've managed to make myself come across as not just upset, but slightly unhinged as well.

"I don't know the details of what's happening between you and Randy, but don't be too hard on yourself," my mom offers gently.

My jaw drops. "What?" What does she mean? What does she think she knows? Does it say, "I'm having sex with Randy Thorn" on my forehead?

My eyes are wide with surprise and confusion. There's a flurry of thoughts and questions I want to unleash, starting with why my mom sounds like she and Randy are old friends.

"There's chemistry—that's all," my mom says, exchanging a knowing look with my dad, who seems to find the situation endearingly amusing.

"There's no chemistry," I retort, feeling a bit defensive.

My dad leans in, offering a reassuring presence. "Everything's going to be okay, Love Bug."

I'm on the verge of questioning, "What do you mean by 'it's okay?'" but I halt, realizing that more protest will only confirm their suspicions.

Taking a moment to collect myself, I breathe deeply, finding clarity in silence. When I speak next, I shift the focus. "Mom, diving back into comedy is incredible. You're truly my inspiration." Then I turn to my dad. "And Dad, retiring to embark on this new adventure with Mom is fantastic. You've always been her biggest supporter, even organizing stand-up sessions for your patients. That was amazing!"

My mom, catching on to my tactic, leans forward with a playful accusation. "Oh, so we're switching topics now?"

I can't help but grimace. "Was it that obvious?"

"Painfully," she teases. "I taught you to be smoother than that," she adds with a wink.

I can't help but laugh, conceding with a playful groan as I go back to my beef stroganoff. "Fine, I admit it. There's something going on with Randy. But I'm dealing with it."

My admission prompts a silent exchange between my parents—a nod from Mom, returned by Dad—signaling their unified support, no matter the topic at hand.

"Whatever's clever," my mom quips with a gentle smile.

"And Gina," my dad interjects, drawing our

attention with his serious tone—a natural command that silences the room. "You are a unique kind of woman, exactly what your mother and I hoped for. You're not someone who can be easily understood. And trust me, Randy is both fascinated and frustrated by that fact." He then looks lovingly at my mom. "The challenge and reward of loving a truly remarkable woman is one of the greatest joys of my life."

Mom responds by blowing him a kiss. "Likewise."

They share a moment of silent communication, their affection evident. Then, shifting his gaze back to me, my dad continues. "All right. Now that we've addressed that, let me share the plans for our first podcast episode and how you can be involved."

CHAPTER 7

The Right Ask

GINA

"AM I really using too much flour and causing trouble for Calypso?" I ask Kai while we're busy with the baking.

He laughs. "No way!" He has to raise his voice a bit over the loud mixer. "Is Randy the one making you worry about this?"

"Yes!" It's such a relief that he figured out the problem right away—it's Randy. Finally, someone gets what I've been going through. "He's always on my case."

Kai turns off the mixer, giving us some peace, and I follow him around the kitchen like an eager puppy. Kai's always on the move, never in one place for too long. "He's got a crush on you, Gina.

Bugging you is just his weird way of trying to get your attention."

"What?" My voice pitches high in surprise as I lean over Kai, who's stooping to grab a melting pot. "You know, Sarah said the same thing recently. But I'm not convinced, especially not now."

Kai, busy with his task, laments the absence of a tempering machine for melting chocolate, noting how much easier and quicker it would make the process. "All Steve needs to do is get one. It wouldn't cost much, all things considered..." He trails off, focusing on measuring chocolate into the pot before looking up at me. "What did you mean by 'especially now'?"

"Are you making the chocolate Ceylon cinnamon rolls?" I ask.

"Yep," he responds, dropping unsweetened chocolate wafers into the pot.

I move toward the metal racks to fetch the glass bin of walnuts. "I'll roast the nuts."

"Thanks," he says.

"But to answer your last question, Randy was on a date Friday night. He's seeing someone." Admitting this out loud feels like taking a punch to the gut.

Kai takes a rare break, narrowing an eye to regard me thoughtfully. "Humph," he finally says.

"Humph?" I echo, desperately wanting to know what he means.

"Yeah, humph," he repeats.

"Okay..."

"Randy doesn't date," he says, sounding sure of himself as he starts stirring the melting chocolate.

Puzzled and a bit unsettled by Kai's assertion, I can't help but frown. I know he must be mistaken; after all, I've witnessed Randy on a date myself. Yet Kai's confidence almost makes me believe him. "Why do you say that?" I press.

Kai gives me a look, his lips twitching as if he's wrestling with whether to share more. The moment stretches, filled with anticipation as I wait for him to elaborate.

Just then, Rita interrupts, peeking into the kitchen. "Gina, your presence is requested at the register."

I reluctantly rip my attention away from Kai, even though I desperately still want to hear what he has to say. But by the time I glance toward the doorway, Rita has already disappeared, leaving me unable to ask who's looking for me.

With a pointed look and a raised finger, I say to

Kai, "I'll be right back," eluding to him that our discussion is far from over.

Kai's nonchalant shrug as he turns back to his work tells me all I need to know. Drawing him back into the conversation about Randy will be a challenge. Nevertheless, as I make my way to the front of the restaurant, my mind buzzes with strategies to revisit the topic. Yet all my planning screeches to a halt the moment I see who's standing in front of the counter, waiting for me. The sight of Randy makes me stop in my tracks. Even my jaw has dropped from sheer shock.

Seeing Randy in casual attire is a rare treat. I've only glimpsed him like this a few times, Friday night included. He has a way of making an edgy black leather jacket look like it was tailored just for him, and today is no exception. Underneath, he sports a frosty pumpkin orange T-shirt that looks impossibly soft. While the counter obscures the rest of his outfit, I'm willing to bet his pants complement his build just as well. Randy's physique is noteworthy, both in and out of his clothes, and the intent way he's looking at me now only adds to his appeal. I've seen that look before, one that usually inspires us both to get half naked and on the kitchen counter.

"No, Gina, no," Naomi's voice says in my head.

And she's right. He's not getting any more of that from me.

Wiping my damp hands on my apron, I steady myself. I'm silently hoping Randy hasn't summoned me from the kitchen to start an argument with me. I'm not ready to go to battle with him just yet.

"I guess you're the one who called me up here?" I ask as I approach him. The familiar scent that's so uniquely Randy washes over me, accompanied by that magnetic pull he always seems to inspire. A shiver runs through me, prompted by our proximity. Realizing I'm too close for comfort, I instinctively step back. Some space between us is definitely required.

A playful yet enticing smirk blossoms on his sexy mouth. "Didn't I see you at the pier with Jeremy the other night?"

"No," I answer too quickly, my response tinged with nervousness I can't quite hide.

Randy's gaze lingers on my face, a hint of curiosity in his eyes. "Jeremy mentioned you took off after spotting me. He was concerned and tried calling, but you didn't pick up."

Internally, I feel like I'm turning to stone. This is the first time I've found myself at a loss for words around Randy, and it's unsettling. Normally, I'm ready with a retort for anything he might throw my way, but this vulnerability, this inability to engage as I usually would, places me at a stark disadvantage.

Struggling for an explanation, I manage, "Umm… I was at my parents' house, so I couldn't answer my phone."

Randy rubs his stubble thoughtfully, nodding as if piecing things together. "Ah, dinner with your parents. I see."

"I'll call him back soon," I assure him, hoping to ease any concern.

At this, his eyebrows knit together. "By the way, the person you saw me with? That was my manager."

"Your manager?" The revelation catches me off guard.

"Yes, the woman you saw me with is my manager—Deanna Blume." He's still grinning like he knows seeing them together has driven me crazy, literally.

Surprise leaves my mouth agape even as a wave of relief turns my once hardened insides into jelly. The impulse to abandon my decision to end things with Randy flares up, yet I resist, knowing it's not wise to flip-flop based on this one clarification. Sure, the woman was his manager this time, but what about next time? What happens when he's on a date with someone else?

However, his mention of having a manager piques my curiosity, stirring an unexpected concern within me. "Why do you need a manager?" I find myself asking.

I note his nonchalant stance, hands tucked into his pockets, as he casually explains. "Because I'm a chef. Even though I've been stationed here for a bit, I haven't given up on my career ambitions just yet."

I bite my tongue because my first instinct is to be sarcastic by rolling my eyes and saying something like, "Yeah, right, Mr. Celebrity Chef," which would've been unnecessarily unkind of me.

Meanwhile, two women by the register are casting flirtatious smiles and batting their eyelashes at Randy. One of them, her voice dripping with sweetness, inquires, "You're Randy Thorn, aren't you?"

Jeez, I think I just caught a sugar high.

"Yes," Randy replies, his response brief yet polite. Then, turning to me, he suggests, "Gina, can we talk over there?" He gestures toward a more secluded spot at the end of the counter.

I give a nod, silently agreeing, and start to follow him. There's something about his demeanor that's very different this time. I have no idea what he has to say to me in private if he's not going to reprimand me about something I did or didn't do.

"Listen," Randy begins, cutting off any chance I have to craft a witty remark to temper the whirlwind of anxiety inside me. There's a peculiar sense that we're on the verge of entering new territory in our interaction. Gosh, he's being too different, and I can't shake the feeling that he's also nervous. But why? Randy Thorn, nervous around me?

"Jeremy mentioned you've been asking him quite a few questions about me. If you have questions, why not come directly to me?"

The answer comes to me swiftly. "Because up until now, you've been nothing but an asshole to me."

His response is to narrow his eyes, but the look he gives me is unexpectedly alluring. "Oh, I've been a lot more to you than just that."

Ooh… His tone is doing things to me. Things I will not let happen anymore. Determined to make my stance crystal clear, I grip the counter and lean in closer, ensuring he won't miss a single word. "Oh, we're done with that."

His steady gaze on me, accompanied by continuous nods, unsettles me, especially when he licks his lips—a gesture that inspires an intense desire to kiss him, which is not exactly what I should be feeling if I want to keep things casual.

"How about I make you dinner tonight?" he proposes after the pause.

My eyes widen in disbelief. "Really?"

I mean, did Randy just ask me out? No, it's not a formal date. He mentioned making dinner, but that's essentially a date, isn't it?

"Yes, Gina. Really." His tone was oh so seductive, and that leaves me speechless.

Then Randy gestures toward the kitchen, holding up a white cloth bag. "I'm going to go into the kitchen with this," he explains, "and make you dinner. After this place closes, it'll just be you and me. You can ask me anything that's on your mind. What do you say?"

CHAPTER 8

The Only Date That Will Ever Matter

GINA

AS RANDY GET to work in the kitchen, whispers start circulating among the customers, wondering if the five-star chef's entrée is on the menu tonight. Whatever Randy is cooking up smells divine.

"Only for one fortunate lady," Rita croons with a beaming smile, giving me a playfully flirtatious look.

For some reason, her comment sent me seeking refuge outside. I needed some fresh air and a moment to gather my thoughts, so I called Naomi. It's such a comfort to know I have a friend who's there for me anytime, anywhere. Naomi was at a dinner with Derek, but she still answered my call.

"I mean, this is not how I pictured things

turning out," I confessed, my voice revealing how worried I was.

"Why not, Gina?" Naomi prodded gently. "Maybe all this time, Randy's been trying to figure out what you really want. So what is it that you want?"

My eyes drifted across the cars cruising down First Street and the birch trees dotting the parking lot. This small town, where I've spent so many years, always carried a quiet melancholy—until Randy burst into my life, stirring everything up. Honestly, before him, I was content to sideline thoughts of romance until I had finished culinary school and mapped out my future. But now, with him preparing dinner for me, my mind swirls with a whirlwind of what-ifs, like the tantalizing yet terrifying prospect of falling for him.

"I don't know," I finally conceded.

"Yes, you do," Naomi insisted gently, her words nudging me to dig deeper for an answer. "You want to be loved. Isn't that what we're all searching for? To be loved?"

"I guess so," I muttered, scuffing the toes of my shoes against the concrete.

"Then be open, relax, and let whatever happens happen," she said.

Naomi's parting advice lingered with me as I deliberately steered clear of the kitchen, where Randy was surprisingly still holed up. It was probably the first time he hadn't emerged to tease or provoke me somehow. A few hours before closing, Rita suggested I head home to change into something more fitting for what she called my "first date" with Randy.

Curious, I asked Rita if she'd been in on Randy's plan to make me dinner since our shift started. Her response was immediate and characteristically honest. "You know I can't keep a secret to save my life."

I couldn't help but laugh. "No, you really can't."

"But just a few minutes ago, he suggested that you might want to go home and change into something more suitable for the occasion. He wants this to feel like a real date for you," Rita said, her eyebrows dancing with excitement at the prospect of Randy and I becoming a real couple.

The thought that Randy had considered this detail warmed me. And so, with a huge smile and the words, "Ten-four," I headed home to get changed.

After a fashion show of my own, trying on no less than nine different outfits, I finally decided on a chic ensemble: a black pencil skirt that fell just below my knees, paired with a sleek black silk camisole. I topped it off with my version of a moto jacket—a nod to the kind of jacket Randy wore today.

When I walked into the Calypso, the transformation of the main dining room took my breath away. The lights were softly dimmed, casting a warm, inviting glow over the room. In the middle of the cleared floor space was a single round table elegantly set with a gold silk tablecloth and two chairs. The centerpiece was a tall, slim white candle, its flame dancing gently in the quiet room. I couldn't help but pause to soak in the romantic setting.

Then, Rita approached me and gave me a warm and reassuring embrace. "Have a wonderful night," she whispered and then winked at me with a twinkle in her eyes. Before departing, she added, "And it's about time this happened."

My eyebrows shot up as I thought, *really?* I guess I had been deluding myself. It seems everybody sensed the unmistakable chemistry between Randy and me after all.

Now, with the doors of Calypso Café securely closed, it's just Randy and me, alone in the establishment. We're seated across from each other, and he has already presented our first course of the night: a beautifully arranged carpaccio of beetroot with goat cheese, candied walnuts, and arugula, all drizzled with aged balsamic vinegar. The presentation is nothing short of artistic, a testament to Randy's culinary expertise. And his face? Bathed in the candle's soft glow, he looks even more handsome than usual, if that's even possible.

So," Randy begins, breaking the silence that had settled after our pleasantries and savoring our first bites, "what do you want to know about me?"

There's one question that's been burning in my mind ever since that first night, the night passion consumed us and we surrendered to it completely. I remember tracing the lines of his tattoo with my tongue, curiosity mingling with yearning.

"The tattoo on your arm," I say. "What does it mean?"

Randy pauses, giving the question the weight it deserves. He slowly sets down his fork and glances at his forearm as if seeing the tattoo anew. "Before I came to this town and started working here, I lived in a sober living house in New York City," he reveals, pausing momentarily to let the significance of his words sink in.

"I didn't know that," I admit, pressing a hand against my heart, which feels like it's trying to beat its way out of my chest. Randy, with his usual confident posture and imposing presence, suddenly appears in a different light. To me, he's always seemed larger than life—almost as if he existed on a different plane from the rest of us. But now, even though he's still so otherworldly, I feel as if I can reach out and touch him.

"Hardly anybody does," he says quietly. "And now you do."

I mirror his half-smile, an attempt to lighten the gravity of the confession.

The atmosphere feels heavier, laden with significance, as he gently runs his finger over his tattoo. "I was a raging drunk," he confesses, "until I lost every last bit of dignity I had."

As Randy's finger lingers on his tattoo, it's clear he's navigating through a sea of memories. "The thing is," he continues, a distant look clouding his eyes, "that wasn't my first attempt to tackle my addiction. When you're famous, even if you find yourself waking up in the gutter, there's a part of you that still believes you've made it. You think you're at the pinnacle of happiness and health. And I was on top of the world, Gina. I was a two-time

James Beard award winner and a Michelin-starred chef."

A heavy silence falls between us, during which I find a lump forming in my throat. The urge to kiss him, to pull him back from the precipice of his past sorrows, is overwhelming.

His voice barely above a whisper now. "Sometimes it felt surreal, like an out-of-body experience, when a room full of my peers would applaud me for a meal that inspired them. But their praise… it never healed me the way I hoped it would."

Leaning forward, a pressing question forms on my lips, driven by a mix of curiosity and concern. "What led you down that path? Do you know?" The depths of his experience feel so foreign to me.

Randy meets my question with a thoughtful nod. "Yes, I finally understand."

My silent attentiveness seems to open the door for him to delve deeper, which he gratefully does.

He shares a pivotal moment from his childhood. At the tender age of ten, he endured the unimaginable loss of his parents in a head-on collision on the interstate. They were returning home from a rare date night in Boston. Subsequently, at eleven, Randy found a new home with Steve's family. His life took a turn as he adjusted to a parenting style vastly different from what he had known with his own parents.

"My uncle's philosophy was that toughness equated to strength, that being hard was what made you a man. My dad couldn't have been more different."

This revelation sheds light on Steve's own struggles, hinting at why he often seems so hard on himself. I remember something happened one day—though the details are fuzzy now—I think he forgot to place an order. He berated himself, saying, "I'm such a bonafide idiot." I was taken aback by that. Instinctively, I responded, "You're not an idiot, Steve. You just forgot." But he looked at me as if my words couldn't penetrate the negative narrative he had about himself. I want to share this memory with Randy, but I hesitate, not wanting to interrupt him.

Randy's gaze shifts away, a shadow of pain crossing his features. "I was just a kid, suddenly without the world I knew. It was as if my uncle and aunt couldn't recognize that. Who demands an eleven-year-old to 'suck it up and be a man'? But that was my uncle's way: you bear it all, silently, 'like a man.'"

Noticing his use of past tense, I probe gently,

"You keep saying 'was'?" It's a subtle question, but I know Randy will grasp the depth of what I'm asking.

"He passed away three years ago, esophagus cancer."

I find myself softly responding, "Oh, I'm so sorry to hear that."

"Me too. Todd was a tough guy—that was his name, Todd. But I loved him, even if it was hard to live under the same roof. That's why, at fifteen, I packed my bags, hopped on a train to New York City, and vowed never to come back. The problem was, I didn't realize that running away doesn't leave your demons behind."

I'm suddenly unable to continue eating my salad. An overwhelming sense of anxiety and sorrow washes over me as if I'm feeling Randy's emotions at eleven and again at fifteen. This wave of empathy brings tears to my eyes and to the edge of spilling over.

Frozen in place, I listen as Randy describes his initial days in New York City, scrambling for a way to survive. He managed to secure a spot in a hostel with the little money he had but knew he needed to find work quickly. His days were filled with visits to various restaurants, offering his services as a dishwasher. The stumbling block, however, was the need for identification.

"I couldn't just show them my school ID—or at least, I thought I couldn't at first. After a month or two, I realized my uncle wasn't going to take any steps to bring me back home. To him, if I was man enough to run away, then I was man enough to fend for myself."

Randy's voice carries a hint of resilience as he continues. "I won't sugarcoat it—things were tough. But Todd did give me access to some money from my parents' trust. That helped, but I still needed to work."

He shares with me that it was Chef Roy Leland who finally offered him a job in his kitchen.

"You mean *the* Chef Roy Leland, renowned for his elevated American cuisine?" I ask.

His expression lights up with pride as he confirms, "The one and only."

Randy goes on to explain that Chef Leland agreed to hire him, but only during after-school hours. However, a few months into the job, Chef Leland noticed Randy wasn't attending school during the day and confronted him with an ultimatum: be honest about his situation or lose the job. By that point, Randy had grown to love working in

Chef Leland's kitchen, a place where the head chef believed everyone on his team should have the skills to step in as junior chefs when necessary.

In Chef Leland's kitchen, Randy quickly learned the art of using a knife, preparing sauces, and mastering seasonings. He discovered he had a natural talent for cooking. So instead of running scared, Randy took the courageous step of sharing his story with the acclaimed chef, explaining the circumstances that led him to New York City.

"Well, you have to finish high school," the chef insisted.

With Chef Leland's support, Randy enrolled in an online high school program, dedicating the early part of his day to his studies before heading to the restaurant by 4 p.m., often working until the early hours of the morning. Randy found that immersing himself in the culinary world not only provided a sense of purpose but also eased the emotional turmoil that had driven him to tears at night. Unfortunately, he also turned to alcohol as a temporary relief from his anguish.

"I worked in that restaurant for thirteen years. When Leland retired six years ago, his kitchen became mine. But eventually, my battle with alcohol cost me the most prestigious job I'd ever had. I'd lash out at my staff, miss entire nights in the kitchen, even forget essential ingredients, like salt."

Hearing this version of Randy, so at odds with the man in front of me, I could only respond, "That doesn't sound like you at all."

"No. Not anymore," he affirmed, lifting his arm to display his tattoo more prominently. "The sword symbolizes my fight against the demons that have tormented me. The clouds around the sword signify my emergence from the darkness, my ascent from the abyss."

Overwhelmed by a surge of emotion, I instinctively lower my face, trying to shield from Randy the tears that have started cascading down my cheeks. "I'm so sorry," I manage to say, the words barely a whisper. My apology is for more than just the moment—it's for every time I mirrored his own harshness, for the complex mix of resentment and attraction I felt toward him, and for failing to see the truth. Despite his undeniable physical prowess and the kind of magnetism that could rival any big-time movie star, he is, at his core, profoundly human.

"Hey," he murmurs, his voice carrying a comforting tone. The gentle touch of his finger under my chin encourages me to look up, and I can almost feel the warmth of his energy urging me to face him.

Brushing away the tears with the back of my hand, I muster a smile as I meet his gaze. "I'm sorry, really sorry."

"There's no need for apologies, Gina. Yes, my story has its sadness, but I like to believe I'm on the path to something better now." The corners of his mouth lift into that irresistibly sexy smirk of his.

Gosh, he's breathtaking. That look he gives me, where his entire face seems to light up, is captivating. Randy has that kind of appeal that I could happily wake up to day after day. Yet despite this undeniable attraction, there remains an elusive barrier between us, invisible but there.

"Yeah, well," I start, feeling the need to shift the conversation, to find a new rhythm in this moment. "You're an incredible chef. That dinner at Pier 37 on Friday night was great, sure, but the ravioli you made that afternoon? It was something else. It made me realize just how talented you are, and then, suddenly, there you were."

Randy licks his lips, which is definitely the greatest show on earth. "Yeah, and there I was."

"And then I ran away," I add, trying to inject some lightness into the moment with a laugh.

I hoped Randy would join in on the laughter, but instead, he extends his arm across the table, his palm open, inviting me to place my hand in his. I accept, and before I know it, he gently pulls me out of my chair and closer to him, bridging the gap between us with a simple gesture. Turning his body to face me, I know exactly what to do as he hikes my skirt up, and I straddle his lap. Lowering myself on top of him, I feel his hardness pushing into my balmy softness. It's like he's already about to explode.

"Gina," he whispers before his lips find the most sensitive side of my neck. "You look stunning tonight, by the way."

"Thank you," I whisper as his kissing makes my body shudder.

"And you drive me crazy," he announces, still tasting my skin.

His careful, indulgent, and soft mouth sends my head afloat. I'm losing patience, and so is he, because what happens next happens so quickly. Randy and I go up in a flurry of hands, unbuttoning, unzipping, removing, and shifting until…

"Uh!" we both utter as our mouths find each other. And while he's inside me, neither of us can get as close to each other as our hearts desire.

TWENTY MINUTES LATER

We're not rushing this moment; instead, we're taking our time, simply gazing into each other's eyes, allowing the connection between us to deepen at its own pace. Our lips stroke the softness of the other's, and our tongues taste the heat of our breaths. Our lovemaking has never soared to such heights. And now, our arms are wrapped around each other, cheeks pressed against each other, and Randy is shuddering passionately yet tenderly as he arrives at the crescendo of our lovemaking.

"Gina," he whispers close to me.

With my eyes closed, I'm wrestling with a storm of emotions that want to claim Randy as my own. "Yes," I respond, my voice a soft echo of his.

"I'm going to be away for a bit," he shares, his voice carrying a weight I wasn't prepared for.

Startled, I emerge out of my oxytocin-inspired haze and pull back slightly to look into his eyes. "You're what?"

"I've been given an opportunity to compete in a cooking competition show, and I've decided to take it."

I'm staring into his eyes, realizing he's still inside me while telling me this.

"One last screw, huh?" I ask, my shaky voice exposing my aching heart.

Randy looks at me, earnest and sincere. "That's not what this is," he insists. "I never planned for it to end like this."

"End? Are you leaving for good?" I ask, already feeling brokenhearted.

"No," he profoundly proclaims. "That's not what I meant. "I didn't plan for us to be like this before I headed to the competition. Although I wanted it. I always wanted it."

Staring into eyes I've looked into a million times, I realize the truth: I never believed this would happen between us either, not like this. Things between us have always had a way of unfolding spontaneously. But it's clear Randy isn't in a place to consider something as serious as a full-time relationship. With this cooking competition, his future has just become a canvas of possibilities—Paris, London, LA, or maybe a return to New York. The world is his oyster.

As for me, I'm still trying to figure out what I truly want from life, where my own path should lead.

"What are you thinking?" His question pulls me from my introspection.

I lock eyes with him, my heart heavy. Yet I'm determined not to let that show. "I'm wondering who's going to clock my arrival time now that you'll be gone?" I manage to joke, trying to lighten the mood with a chuckle.

Randy's smile flickers, bittersweet, before he draws me closer, and we find ourselves lost in a series of kisses. Between the tender moments, he murmurs, "Oh no, Chef Emerson, I will never stop being a pain in your ass." His words muffle as our kisses deepen, our connection unspoken yet solid as we continue to explore the comfort and chaos of our emotions.

CHAPTER 9

Journey Men

RANDY

SINCE RETURNING TO MY HOMETOWN, I've been living in the house I grew up in. My Uncle Todd, my father's brother, couldn't bring himself to sell it after my parents died. Todd was a man of contradictions—there were times when a little softness from him could have made a world of difference. Yet in his own way, and when it truly counted, he showed his love—like keeping this house just for me and the family he hoped I would one day make.

Jeremy, having blown into town last week, has been lodging at Steve's place. He would have preferred to stay here with me, but he's here to look after Steve, which makes it all the more disappointing that Steve didn't show up with Jeremy to see me off like he promised.

My flight to New Orleans is in four hours. That's where the Head Chef World Domination competition is being filmed. It's supposed to be a grueling production schedule, lasting somewhere between eight and twelve weeks. I don't want to go that long without seeing Gina, but what am I to do? I can't back out now. But there's something worse that could happen with me being gone for so long, and it has to do with Steve, who isn't here like he should be.

For my last meal with Jeremy, I made something special—our favorite, Oysters Rockefeller, accompanied by spinach and parmesan risotto.

"Damn," Jeremy murmurs, his eyes closed as he savors each bite. "This is like music to my mouth."

His lighthearted approach to the moment irks me, especially considering the circumstances. I'm on the verge of expressing my frustration about Steve's absence yet again, when my phone dings with an incoming message.

I glance at the screen. "It's Steve," I announce, my frown deepening so much that it adds to my headache. "He's in Atlantic City."

"Ah, hell." Jeremy blows out a breath, leaning back in his chair, his demeanor dimming as he fully grasps the situation. The realization of what can happen when Steve is left unsupervised seems to finally hit him.

Rubbing my temples, I try to ease the tension headache building from the stress. Yet despite the unfolding chaos with Steve, I find my usual readiness to lash out dampened by the lingering bliss of my night with Gina. Her taste, her touch, the intimacy we shared—it's all still vivid, casting a glow over everything else. Steve's reckless escapades in Atlantic City can't completely erase this serene afterglow.

"He's a grown man," Jeremy mutters after a while, perhaps more for his own reassurance than mine.

"Yeah, but he's our cousin," I counter, feeling the full gravity of those words.

A heavy silence follows my statement, underscoring the magnitude of the situation. The weight of our shared history, of our responsibility toward one another, feels heavy. Jeremy, Steve, and I—we've looked out for each other since childhood. Steve often bridged the gap between his father and me, stepping in to look after me when needed. The thought solidifies my resolve; I owe it to him to return that care, no matter the cost.

"Shit," I mutter, the importance of the situation

pressing down on me. "Maybe I should call the show and back out."

"The hell you will," Jeremy counters, his determination clear. "You're going. I'll handle Steve. Unless..." His expression shifts to one of speculation. "This hesitation isn't really about Steve, is it?"

Jeremy raises his hands in a gesture of peace. "Hey, I get it. She's the kind of person who could make you reconsider everything. I just wish she wasn't into you."

I give him a pointed look, half-joking, half-serious. "Keep your thoughts—and hands—to yourself while I'm gone."

"So, are you and Gina officially an item now?" Jeremy asks.

Jeremy's probing question sends a wave of anxiety crashing over me. The truth is, I'm navigating uncharted waters here. My passion for cooking has always been my primary focus, relegating any form of human intimacy to nothing more than fleeting encounters. Genuine companionship, the kind that goes beyond the physical, has never been part of my repertoire. Until Gina, I hadn't been with the same woman more than twice, or maybe three times, let alone experienced anything like the intense, all-consuming connection

I felt with her last night. The depth, the slow burn, the reluctance to part ways—it was unfamiliar territory. Was that love? I'm not even sure.

"Are you two together now?" Jeremy presses, snapping me back to the present and nudging me toward an answer.

"I don't know," is all I manage, feeling the weight of uncertainty as I rub the back of my neck.

Jeremy doesn't let up. "Do you like her?"

"Of course."

"She knows you're leaving?"

"Yeah."

"What did she say about it?"

I pause, leaning back and fixing Jeremy with a wary look. "Why the interrogation?"

He chuckles, shrugging it off. "Just curious, that's all. I mean, I would've appreciated a heads-up that you two have been together for quite a while, but don't worry, man. I'd never step into something you've got going on. You know that."

I nod, reassured by his words. "I know that."

"However," Jeremy continues, his tone shifting as he raises a finger for emphasis. "The moment you decide you're not pursuing that route anymore, give me a heads-up. I wouldn't mind trying my luck with her again."

I'm left speechless by his audacity, my emotions fluctuating between irritation and disbelief. Before I can gather my thoughts, Jeremy bursts out laughing, clapping his hands in amusement.

"You should see your face," he teases, barely containing his amusement. "Man, you're in love with her."

Despite my instinct to deny it, I find myself unable to outright refute his observation. "I feel things for Gina," I concede, a mix of confusion and realization in my voice. "I have deep feelings for her. But whether this is love or just another form of addiction, I can't say for sure."

The laughter fades from Jeremy's face, replaced by a look of earnest concern. He understands the journey I've undergone to arrive at this point, the battles fought to stand here, perhaps not entirely whole, but certainly less fractured than before. Leaning in, he plants his elbows on the table, ensuring we're eye to eye, signaling the gravity of his words.

"Don't worry about Gina," he begins, his voice steady and sincere. "I'll keep an eye on her for you and my hands to myself. I promise. I'll also take care of Steve and make sure he doesn't lose his shirt at the casino. Your only focus should be on winning that competition. Because Randy, you're an exceptional chef and an incredible cousin. And when you're ready, you'll be an amazing partner for someone. Especially for a woman as remarkable as Gina. She's exactly the kind of person you deserve."

Choked up, I rise to my feet, arms out wide, gesturing for Jeremy to stand for a hug. At this moment, I'm embracing one of the two pillars who have kept me from falling apart. Jeremy and Steve are the reasons I'm still standing. They are why I haven't lost myself to despair. They're why I'm not crying over missed opportunities and a future I've let slip through my fingers.

"I love you," I say with absolute certainty.

Jeremy responds with a kiss on my cheek. "I love you too." He then steps back. "Now, go. You don't want to miss your flight. I'll handle the cleanup here and then head to Atlantic City to sort out Steve."

We exchange a final handshake, pull in for a last tight hug, and then part ways—each of us embarking on our separate paths. I'm off to seize a career-defining opportunity, and Jeremy is off to save Steve from himself.

CHAPTER 10

Without Randy

GINA

TODAY IS JUST another manic Wednesday. Entering the Calypso Café, I can't help but immediately look at the clock above the front counter. Yep, I'm seven minutes late, again. No matter how much I rush, leaving class at 12:35 p.m. just doesn't give me enough time to clock in by 1 p.m.

A certain memory comes to mind, and it's clear as day. It's of Randy watching me from across the room as I walk in. But now I can see something in his eyes I missed before. There was a kind of eagerness, as if he had been looking forward to my arrival. Yet all he got from me was a grumpy frown and a bit of attitude. Looking back, it's so evident that there was more going on between us beneath the surface.

I already miss him—I miss him more than I thought possible.

"Gina!" Sarah calls, pulling me back to the present.

"Hey, Sarah! I'll be right there," I call back, quickening my steps toward the locker room.

"We need you in the kitchen."

I halt, surprised. "In the kitchen?" It's only then that I notice her frantic energy and the bustling scene of the café. Having called in sick yesterday, I was under the impression from Rita that, with Randy's departure, the lunch and dinner rushes would diminish, especially since his signature dishes were supposedly off the menu. Clearly, I was misinformed.

The café before Randy's arrival was a different place. We served simple pastries, sandwiches, salads, and usually closed by 6 p.m. Everything changed when he took charge.

I recall Randy's first staff meeting vividly. He gathered all eleven of us in the break room after hours and announced in a no-nonsense tone that things were going to change. He caught me rolling my eyes at his declaration and gave me a sharp scowl. But my resistance to his new management style didn't end with just an eye roll.

"We're going to serve real food here," he said.

I couldn't help but raise my hand, which earned me a warning glare from him before he said, "Yes…" The tone in his voice beckoned me to introduce myself.

"Gina," I responded, my voice laced with a hint of chill.

"What's your question, Gina?" he asked, echoing the iciness in my tone.

"Are sandwiches, salads, and pastries not real food?"

His gaze intensified, locking with mine. "Is that a rhetorical question you're asking there, Gina, or a hostile one?"

"Both," I admitted, standing my ground.

Randy remained still for a moment, observing me intently, undisturbed, with one foot casually resting on a step stool. What he was thinking during that silent standoff, only he could say. Eventually, he diverted his gaze from mine and continued with the meeting, brushing past my challenge as if it never happened. My defiance was partly fueled by the memories of our previous manager, Rex. Rex was the kind of manager who seemed only interested in his paycheck, often delegating his responsibilities to Sarah. She, being too kindhearted, never pushed back against his laziness. To this day, it puzzles me how Steve ever concluded that Rex was fit to manage a café.

Then, one day, Rex and Steve had a major confrontation right in the middle of the café, in full view of everyone, staff and customers alike. Rex lashed out at Steve, accusing him of potentially gambling the café away someday. In his tirade, Rex didn't hold back, calling Steve a whiny liar and complaining about the low pay—all of which, unfortunately, held some truth. After Rex stormed out and quit, no one stepped in to fill his shoes. Sarah, with her dedication and efficiency, ran the café flawlessly, yet Steve seemed oblivious to her efforts. That's why I was initially upset when Randy arrived, seemingly sidelining Sarah by taking over her duties and demoting her to the role of a cashier.

"We'll be offering the celebrity chef menu," Randy declared to the room.

Without hesitation, my hand went up again, and from the look on Randy's face, it seemed acknowledging me required a monumental effort on his part. "Yes, Gina."

My confusion was genuine as I asked, "Who's the celebrity chef?"

"He's the celebrity chef," Pete chimed in, unable to hide his annoyance at my question.

Feeling somewhat rebuked, I slowly retracted my hand, swallowing the next question that had been on the tip of my tongue.

I remained silent, albeit with difficulty, as Randy outlined his plans to introduce two three-course entree options during dinner hours and two unique "elevated" American cuisine dishes for lunch.

"Elevated?" My voice dripped with skepticism as I crossed my arms, clearly unimpressed.

"Gina, come on," Steve interjected, his irritation evident.

I had almost forgotten he was even present; his appearance at staff meetings was rare. Reflecting on it, he looked exhausted, as if sleep had been elusive for days.

Yet my frustration was at a boiling point. A significant part of my irritation stemmed from Randy's inexplicably attractive presence—it was almost unfair how good-looking our new boss was, making me think he belonged in Hollywood rather than here. So I didn't let up, especially when Randy mentioned that our in-house dining approach wouldn't change, despite the introduction of "elevated" food.

"It's a give and take," he suggested.

"I don't even know what that means," I countered impulsively.

His response came with a curious tilt of his head. "It means, Gina, that we'll be offering pricier menu options but with lower operational costs."

Unsatisfied, I tilted my head, bracing for a confrontation. "But won't that mean more profit? Unless your plan is to increase revenue at the expense of the staff's workload."

The silence that followed my challenge was telling; not a single murmur or sigh broke the quiet. The tension in the room was thick, and you could hear a pin drop as everyone waited for Randy's response.

When Randy glanced at Steve, I immediately grasped the underlying message. Steve's gambling issues weren't a secret, and the look of concern on Randy's face wasn't lost on me. He was here with a purpose—to turn the café's finances around swiftly. While Randy would never openly admit it, it was clear that Steve's debts, likely to some unsavory characters from Boston, were a pressing issue. The kind of men who would come looking for Steve at the café were not the sort to engage in pleasantries. Their avoidance of eye contact wasn't out of shyness but a deliberate attempt to keep their dealings cold and impersonal.

"Forget it," I finally conceded, dropping my arms. "Go on."

Randy paused for a moment, giving me a look that felt like a silent thank-you for easing up on him. Yet I could tell he was still keeping a close eye on me. The very next day, my habitual Wednesday lateness got me summoned to his office for a talk about how important it is to be punctual. We ended up in a heated debate, the tension between us like the north and south poles of magnets. It was as if there was this strange, intense pull drawing us together, almost pushing us to act on it right then and there—and we almost did.

Frankly, not much had changed between Randy and me until Sunday night. Our tender time together stretched into the wee hours of Monday. That night, our connection deepened in a way I hadn't anticipated. We made love with a gentle, unhurried intensity, clinging to each other as if letting go was unthinkable. When we weren't lost in the slow rhythm of our bodies, our kisses filled the spaces between, their depths making me dizzy. I found myself memorizing the feel of his skin under my lips, covering every inch of his face and neck with kisses, and he reciprocated with equal fervor. The truth was, neither of us wanted to break that bond. Neither of us wanted to be separated from the intimate closeness we'd unexpectedly found in each other.

It wasn't until around four in the morning that we finally settled down to finish eating his meticulously prepared filet mignon, accompanied by truffle mashed potatoes and roasted artichoke hearts lightly drizzled with lemon and olive oil. By then, we had migrated to the small sofa in Steve's office. As I sat in Randy's lap, we reminisced about all the times we had clashed over trivial matters, laughing over past disputes.

Being together in such a candid, intimate manner was incredibly fulfilling, yet we were aware that the clock was ticking and our time was limited. Pete had been given the night off to afford Randy and me this special opportunity, and we knew Kai would be arriving by 5 a.m. to start the day's baking. Acknowledging the approaching dawn, we shared one final, fervent kiss, a perfect culmination of our night together. I offered him my best wishes for the cooking competition, and we said our final goodbyes. I left feeling a surge of optimism, which was unlike anything I'd ever felt before. Driving home, it felt as though I could soar. In that moment, I entertained the possibility—no, I embraced the feeling—that I might truly be in love with Randy Thorn.

Later that day, Randy called from the airport just before his flight boarded. I missed it because I was deep in sleep, recovering from our intense night. I replayed his message back several times. He talked about our unforgettable night, mentioned he would miss me, and expressed a desire to see me again upon his return, promising to call soon. Despite my attempts to return his call, my efforts went straight to voicemail. But I'm still eagerly waiting for him to get in touch when he finds a moment.

He's still heavy on my mind as I rush through the ritual of stowing away my things in the locker room and slipping into an apron. Once I'm ready to start my shift, I make my way into the kitchen, not sure of what to expect. And there, to my surprise, is Jeremy.

CHAPTER 11

The New Cook

GINA

"HEY," I say tightly, unable to move a muscle.

Unsurprisingly, Jeremy is impeccably dressed. He's wearing well-tailored dress pants paired with a crisp, gray button-down shirt, the sleeves casually rolled up to his elbows, adding a touch of effortless elegance. Given our last encounter on the docks and how I've gone silent on him by neither answering nor returning any of his calls, his presence catches me off guard. Despite this, he greets me with a pleasant, welcoming smile, a kindness that I feel utterly unworthy of.

"Hi, Gina. This is for you." He hands me a binder. "You're the only person Randy trusts with these."

I'm rendered immobilized for a moment.

Touching something that belongs to Randy almost feels like a much-wanted hug from him. Then I open the binder and see that it contains Randy's celebrity chef entree recipes. As I thumb through the pages, I'm struck by the meticulous attention to detail each recipe showcases.

"I thought these offerings were being discontinued," I comment.

Jeremy's response is a telling silence, prompting me to glance up from reading Randy's brown butter lamb ravioli recipe, my favorite. The grimace on Jeremy's face speaks volumes.

"What is it?" I press, sensing there's more to the story.

"We can't afford to take the financial hit right now," he finally admits.

My mind immediately jumps to the usual suspect. "Is it Steve again?"

He mashes his lips together, signaling he will neither confirm nor deny. He is definitely very loyal to Steve. Randy is the same way.

Jeremy breaks the silence. "Plus, we'll have to let go of some kitchen staff if we don't keep up with the lunch and dinner options. We don't want anyone losing their job."

"I agree," I find myself saying, even though I

suspect the real reason we're continuing with Randy's menu is more about Steve's situation. Working here has always been a bit of a tightrope walk—balancing the fear that Steve's personal issues might one day land us in a precarious situation, possibly under less savory management. Yet there's also the liberating aspect of his hands-off approach, granting us considerable autonomy to excel and genuinely make this place shine. But it's not like Steve gives us free reign of the place on purpose. He's often too preoccupied with his own concerns to be involved in the café's operations.

Jeremy raises his hands in a gesture of peace. "Also, I want you to know that we're good."

Feeling a wave of embarrassment crash over me, I lower my gaze. "Sorry about not calling you back. I meant to, but everything just seemed to happen so fast after that night."

"It's okay, Gina. Stop beating yourself up about it," he says, his voice carrying a tone of understanding as he places a comforting hand on my shoulder. "But it would've been nice if either of you had mentioned something about what was happening between you two. I get it, though. Randy's not exactly the type to share those kinds of things with anyone."

A question sits on the tip of my tongue. But do I really want to know the answer? Actually, I do! "What kind of things are you referring to?" I ask.

Jeremy's response comes with a playful chuckle. "Let's just say those things have something to do with why Randy warned me to keep my distance. And told me not to ask you on any more dates."

My smile broadens uncontrollably, a rush of joy surging through me at this revelation. The thought that Randy cares enough to stake his claim, even in his absence, fills me with an undeniable reassurance that we are definitely in this together. This is fantastic news.

Jeremy analyzes my reaction. "Wow, I never stood a chance in hell, did I?"

Realizing my expression might have been a bit too telling, I quickly try to moderate my smile.

But Jeremy just laughs at my attempt. "All right, Gina, let's see you pull this off," he says, smoothly transitioning the conversation back to the task at hand.

CHAPTER 12

Too Busy To Tell

GINA

SIX WEEKS LATER

Panting, I force out the words, "I'm so out of shape," as I struggle to keep pace with Naomi. My burning lungs protest every effort to keep running.

"Not me," Naomi replies, her voice strained, her face twisted in discomfort.

Our laughs sound like wheezing as it becomes evident that she's in just as much pain as I am.

It feels like an eternity since I last joined Naomi for our regular Sunday morning run at Blue Ridge Park. Since becoming head chef at Calypso, Sundays are now my only days off. My schedule throughout the rest of the week is jam-packed, juggling the demands of the kitchen with my cooking classes. With graduation just a month away, the pressure is mounting. Additionally, there's my parents' podcast. They want me to participate, and despite my tight schedule, I find myself unable to refuse—it's actually enjoyable. I appreciate the extra time with my parents, even if it is a bit startling to see how freely the empty nesters who lunch discuss their kids' private lives on air.

Naomi, now visibly struggling to keep pace, smashes her hands against her waist and gasps out, "Power walk?"

Seizing the lifeline, I manage to wheeze out, "Yes."

Walking is still uncomfortable. My hamstrings scream with tightness, my calves twitch with spasms, and I'm fighting nausea that's been haunting me since this morning. Before joining Naomi on the track, I stopped by the health food store, bought a ginger shot, and downed it. That gave me some relief. But now the sensation has returned, and with alarming intensity.

"So what's been going on with you?" Naomi asks, her breath now steadier.

"Work, school, podcast, sleep," I list, ticking off each item on my fingers as we walk.

Then without missing a beat, she dives into the

topic she's most curious about. "Have you heard from Randy?"

So here's the thing—I've kept the details of my special night with Randy to myself, not even sharing them with Naomi. There was a depth to our connection that evening, a profound intimacy that felt too sacred to immediately share. I wanted to wait and see how our next conversation would unfold when we spoke again.

As time passed, my decision to hold back seems to have been the right call. It has been six weeks, and there's been nothing but silence from Randy's end. No calls, no messages—nothing. And tomorrow, it seems, I can see his face again. The Premiere Eats Channel is airing the first episode of the new season of *Head Chef Total Domination*, and Randy will be on it. The thought of watching him on TV twists my heart a bit. I told myself I could just skip the show and avoid the pain of seeing him while not hearing from him. But who am I kidding? Skipping it isn't really an option. Despite everything, I know I'll be watching, clinging to the screen for a glimpse of his handsomeness.

"Nope, haven't heard a peep from him," I manage to say. The effort of maintaining our brisk pace makes it difficult to converse. "Can we slow down a bit more?"

Naomi immediately adjusts her speed, for which I'm immensely grateful.

She looks at me, her eyebrows knitted with concern. "Are you okay?"

I take a deep breath of the crisp morning air and let it calm my senses slightly. "I am now," I assure her, even though I'm far from okay.

As Naomi pauses, her gaze lingers on me, growing more scrutinizing. I put on an extra effort to appear unbothered, to seem like everything is normal. But the truth is that something has been off for quite some time now.

"So what's been happening with you?" I quickly ask in an attempt to redirect the conversation, hoping to shift her focus away from my uncomfortable life.

"Same old, same old," Naomi says airily. She loops her arm through mine, pulling me closer. "It feels kind of strange that I'm finally graduating from law school, though. It's been two long, grueling years."

I'm finding it increasingly difficult to keep down the banana and bran muffin I ate after the ginger shot, but if I'm being honest with myself, this uneasy feeling isn't new to just this morning. My stomach has felt off for a while now. Perhaps it's something I ate recently that's not agreeing with me. Just last Friday, I recall devouring quite a few tuna tartare bites in an attempt to sustain my energy levels while cooking. The realization of how challenging Randy's job truly is hits me hard. What leaves me puzzled is wondering how he managed to prepare all that food and still find time to get under my skin.

So it's my nausea that's keeping me from congratulating her on making it through.

"But I do have best-girlfriend news to share," she announces.

"Um, okay," I say, struggling not to vomit all over the park's nice, clean track.

"Derek has been offered an opportunity to merge with a top law firm in Boston."

My sudden surprise momentarily relieves my nausea. "What? Are you moving to Boston?" I exclaim, already experiencing the blues that will come if Naomi moves away.

She gently releases her arm from mine, her voice uncertain. "I, we, don't know yet. We're weighing the pros and cons."

Feeling a wave of discomfort, I exhale deeply.

"Well, there are more pros than cons," I start, trying to hide the sadness in my voice. "I don't want you to leave, but Derek is driven, and so are you. Boston offers the opportunities you're both looking for. But still, I don't know what I'll do here without you." The sadness tugs at my smile, turning it downward.

She looks at me with a thoughtful expression. "Can I put my lawyer hat on for a moment? I have a case to make that just might bring us both some hope and optimism." She places a comforting hand on my back.

"I'm all ears," I say, eager for any insight she has to share.

Naomi takes a deep breath. "You know, we haven't seen each other in sixteen days, even though we're in the same town. It's easy to take our time for granted when we're so close. If I move, we'll have to make an effort to see each other. We'll plan visits and make them count. You're my best friend, but you're more my sister, and honestly, I can't imagine a life without Gina in it."

Suddenly, a crippling wave of nausea overwhelms me, forcing me to double over and clutch at my knees for support.

"Gina, what's happening?" Naomi shrieks, her voice thick with worry.

I shut my eyes tight, silently pleading for the discomfort to subside. *Please, let this pass,* I mentally beg, but the nausea refuses to obey. Gripping my stomach, I desperately scan our surroundings until my gaze locks on a trash can along the track. With sheer determination, I propel myself toward it, fighting to keep everything down until I reach it. When I do, I commence puking my guts out.

Naomi quickly runs to her car and comes back with a bottle of cherry-flavored electrolyte water. "Drink all of this," she instructs as we settle on the grass, both of us recovering from my ordeal.

"Gina," she begins, a hint of hesitancy in her voice. "You know I have to ask."

I frown immediately, anticipating her question. "I'm not pregnant, Naomi. It's impossible. I had my period after Randy left."

"And he's the only person you've been with?" she probes further.

"Yes, of course," I respond, feeling a mix of surprise and annoyance. "If there was anyone else, you'd be the first to know."

"Not necessarily," she retorts a bit too swiftly,

her voice tinged with a hint of dissatisfaction with me.

"What are you trying to say?" I press.

"I have this feeling that you're holding back details about you and Randy."

"What?" I ask, alarmed. Why is she always so spot on?

"You couldn't stop talking about him before," she continues. "And now that he's not around, I'm hearing nothing from you."

"Maybe now that he's gone, there's nothing more to say."

"Maybe. I just..." She trails off, her expression one of confusion and frustration. "Never mind. Let's drop it."

A heavy silence ensues, thick with things left unsaid. Part of me wants to come clean about that last night with Randy, to confirm her suspicions. Yet I find myself hesitating. Why hasn't he reached out like he promised?

Opting for a safer topic, I say, "I think it's the tuna tartare puffs I ate too many of while cooking in the kitchen on Friday night."

Naomi nods, her response brimming with certainty. "That makes sense. Raw fish can be tricky."

I offer a weak smile in agreement. "I know, right?" But internally, I'm grappling with doubts. The truth is, whatever caused my sickness didn't taste anything like tuna tartare.

THE NEXT DAY

This morning, I was sick again, leaving me in a state of uncertainty about my health. With my schedule as packed as it is, there's hardly any time to pause and figure out what's wrong. One thing I'm sure of, however, is that it can't possibly be pregnancy—I had my period a few days after that unforgettable night with Randy. It wasn't as heavy as usual, but it was definitely there.

While driving to class, my health improved, and my focus shifted to the impending cooking exam—a test that was about to start in seconds. My performance on the previous two cooking exams was exceptional. I attribute it to the skills I honed during my brief tenure as a chef at Calypso. Cooking under pressure has become second nature to me. I sweat like crazy trying to get food on the plate in a timely manner. Thankfully, Randy trained his kitchen staff well. Without them, I would've given up by now. Also, my love for baking has allowed me to creatively incorporate those elements into my exam entrees, a strategy that I believe has significantly contributed to my high scores.

In the classroom, fifteen of us stand by our stations. Anticipation hangs heavily in the air. Before each of us lies a large bowl filled with green, red, orange, and red bell peppers, which are our focus ingredients for this exam. Our task is to craft a breakfast dish, skillfully weaving these peppers into our creations.

Chef Nelson, our instructor, positions himself near the timer switch that will set us in motion. "You have an hour to prepare your dish. Make it presentable and flavorful," he announces.

As the moment to begin ticks closer, time seems to suspend, leaving us all in a state of heightened readiness, eager to dive into the task at hand. However, amidst this tension, a sudden scent wafts through the air, striking an uneasy chord within me. My stomach churns in protest, and I fight the overwhelming urge to be sick once more.

I fix my gaze on the culprit—it's the scent of the green bell pepper. *No, no, no, no,* races through my mind as the feeling of sickness intensifies, threatening to consume me.

With the competition underway, leaving my station to rush to the bathroom isn't an option. Nor can I afford to lose focus on crafting a dish that not only uses the peppers but also weaves in an element of fresh baking. Determined, I shut my eyes for a moment, willing away the nausea with sheer force of will.

The sound of the timer starting snaps my eyes open. "Start," announces the electronic voice, following Chef Nelson's activation of the countdown.

Now I have no choice but to ignore my discomfort by joining the scramble toward the cooler with my classmates. The space around me becomes a flurry of activity, hands reaching, bodies bumping, and a chorus of polite "excuse me's" filling the air. My mind is already racing with plans for my dish—pan-seared salmon with a poached egg crowned with a richly flavored roasted pepper puree.

The intensity of the competition pushes my nausea aside for now. Focused, I start by preparing my peppers for roasting. I coat them in a mixture of butter, cinnamon, cloves, smoked paprika, and honey, then I slide them into the oven to roast.

Next, I turn my attention to the soda bread dough. I believe in the power of homemade bread to elevate a dish. I plan to use the bread as the base for the other components. Next, I make a glaze of brown butter and honey for a crispy finish on my salmon.

"Thirty minutes," announces the automated timer, reminding me of the fleeting time.

The tension escalates. Blenders, mixers, sizing, and clanking utensils fill the air. My bread is taking on a golden hue in the oven, signaling that it's nearly time to focus on the ricotta. Amid the hustle and the heat that's settling around us, I find myself in the zone. Testing the ricotta's texture with a swipe of my finger, I confirm it's precisely as it should be.

Suddenly, I change my plan and abandon the idea of adding a poached egg to my dish. I cannot risk having any element overpower the harmony of flavors that I intend for Chef Nelson to appreciate.

After just twenty minutes, the peppers have become a smooth puree, perfectly seasoned to complement the honey-glazed crackling layering my seared salmon. Now it's time to plate.

"Five minutes," the timer voices.

"I execute my next steps with precision. First, I

cut a perfect slice of bread, toast it lightly for texture, and then shape it into a flawless circle. Then I artfully smear a foundation of pepper sauce on the plate, upon which I place the toast. Finally, I crown it with freshly made ricotta."

"Two minutes!" echoes in the kitchen, ramping up the pressure.

I gently arrange a piece of the tender, flaky salmon on top of the ricotta, finishing with an additional drizzle of the vibrant sauce.

A final inspection and clean-up of my plate are completed just as the timer announces the end by buzzing.

Time's up!

FIFTEEN MINUTES LATER

Chef Nelson moves methodically through the room, evaluating each student's culinary creations with a discerning eye. The grading process seems unpredictable as he navigates from one station to the next, occasionally bypassing a few before returning. His approach keeps everyone on their toes, unsure of when their turn will come.

I'm getting antsy because now that the bustle of cooking and plating is over, my adrenaline rush is subsiding. That sick feeling nips at my stomach again. I cast an anxious glance at the clock, silently pleading for Chef Nelson to please hurry. The thought of needing to excuse myself before receiving his feedback is unbearable, both as a matter of personal pride and professional decorum.

As my sickness intensifies, desperation sets in. I scan the classroom for the nearest trash can, readying myself for the inevitable. The feeling of nausea becomes so overpowering that the fear of embarrassment fades into insignificance. I close my eyes, sway slightly, and silently plead for Chef Nelson to hurry up.

At long last, Chef Nelson approaches my station, making me his final stop for the day.

"You baked again?" he inquires, an eyebrow arching inquisitively.

"Yes, Chef," I manage to say, hoping my urgency isn't too apparent.

He leans in to smell my dish, and a moment of suspense hangs in the air. "Once again, you've managed to turn what could have been ordinary into a savory dessert," he observes.

I muster a tight smile, silently pleading with my body to hold itself together for just a little longer.

He bends over and studies my plate before

slicing through my entree with his fork. "Nice," he compliments.

Chef Nelson artfully swirls his bite through the sauce on the plate and then places it in his mouth. My heart pounds as his jaw churns.

"This sauce is magnificent, Chef," he comments, and then he goes for a second bite—a promising sign. It's widely recognized among us students that while a single taste is usually enough for him to judge a dish, he tends to indulge in a few more bites when he's particularly impressed.

He helps himself to another portion, noting, "Your fish is flaky, bread baked to perfection, and..."

But before he can finish his praise, and before I have the chance to modestly reply, "Thank you, Chef," the overwhelming urge to puke takes over. With no time to spare, I dash as quickly as I can to the nearest trash can—right beside his teaching station. I feel everyone watching as I succumb to my nausea, unable to contain it any longer

CHAPTER 13

All The Tests in The World

GINA

The weight of my exhaustion is evident as I trudge into the Calypso, each step feeling heavier than the last.

"Eek!" Sarah's voice pierces the air just as I'm stepping farther into the café. "Gina, good news."

Gratefully, I pause, seizing the chance to rest, even if just for a moment. Standing here, I feel as though I could collapse into sleep without warning.

"We're scaling back to only offering the celebrity chef specials on Fridays and Saturdays. So you can head home because..." Her expression softens into one of genuine concern. "You look absolutely worn out."

"What? How?" is all I manage to stammer out in my confusion.

My mouth drops open in astonishment, struggling to process Sarah's rapid-fire explanation. At first, her words float around me, disjointed and distant. But then her words start to crystalize, forming a coherent message.

With a gesture of genuine care, Sarah gently grips my shoulders, her words pouring out in a hurried stream. "Gina, you've been pushing yourself to the limit here. Between managing the kitchen, attending school, and contributing to the podcast—which, by the way, you're amazing at—it's just too much. I couldn't stand by and watch you run yourself into the ground. You're fading away right before our eyes, and it's got all of us worried sick. So I reached out to Jeremy and Steve. Steve was unreachable, but Jeremy picked up right away. I shared my worries with him, and he was immediately on board. He agreed that limiting the chef specials to Friday and Saturday was a sensible move. He even mentioned that if this adjustment doesn't help ease your burden, we could consider dropping the specials altogether."

The revelation leaves me utterly astonished, yet a profound sense of relief washes over me. Questions swirl in the recesses of my mind, yet I find myself unable to articulate them. At this moment, the only response I can muster is emotional as tears of relief well up in my eyes. Without a word, I pull Sarah into a grateful embrace, my heart swelling with gratitude for her intervention. As I bid farewell to my coworkers, their goodbyes echoing warmly behind me, I head to my car, still in a daze from the unexpected turn of events.

The drive home is brief, but it's a struggle to keep my eyes open and my focus sharp. The exhaustion that has accumulated over weeks, perhaps months, of pushing myself too hard is ready to claim me. Every red light feels like an invitation to close my eyes, and the familiar streets seem to stretch on longer than usual. The thought of my bed, of finally allowing myself to rest without the weight of immediate responsibilities, propels me forward. I urge myself to stay awake until, finally, I'm home.

The moment I cross the threshold of my apartment, my body gives in to exhaustion. I collapse onto the sofa, curl up, and draw myself into the tightest ball possible. Almost immediately, sleep overtakes me.

Awakening later, I'm disoriented by the darkness enveloping the room. The pressing need for a bathroom visit momentarily pulls me back to reality, yet my mind is consumed by a single thought: *Head Chef Total Domination.* The mere idea of seeing Randy on my TV screen stirs a mix of anticipation and unease, yet I can't resist the pull.

I go quickly to relieve my bladder and then return to switch on the television. The digital clock in the corner of the screen catches my eye—it's 11:32 p.m., long after the show's 6 p.m. airtime. But that's no matter; I had the foresight to set my DVR to record the entire series.

Without hesitation, I reach for the remote control on the coffee table. Just as I'm about to turn on the TV, a sharp cramp in my stomach stops me in my tracks. Clenching my hands into fists, I can't help but feel a sense of triumph. "Yes," I whisper to myself, believing that my period has finally started. Grinning happily, I'm sure all I needed was some much-needed rest to get my cycle back on track.

Quickly, I head back to the bathroom, pull down my pants, and reach for some toilet paper. My heart sinks as I look down. My initial relief turns to dismay. "Shoot," I mutter to myself, staring in disbelief at the toilet paper. There's not even a dot of blood.

Frustrated and confused, I let out a sigh and press my face into my hands. The cramps I felt were unmistakable, usually a sure sign that my period is imminent. Then again, nausea hasn't been my only symptom lately. I've also had tenderness in my breasts. Standing up, I pull my pants back up and walk into my bedroom, feeling restless. I contemplate just going to sleep, hoping to wake to the start of my cycle, yet the uncertainty gnaws at me. Why delay when I could have clarity right now?

With a newfound resolve, I stride back to the living room, snatch my keys from the wall hook near the door, and grab my purse from the sofa. My drive to the drugstore is tense. My hands tremble as they grip the steering wheel, my mind awash with worry. I try to recall the last time I had my birth control injection. Was it just two weeks before the semester began, or has it been two months? Perhaps a month and a half? With everything that's been going on, it's hard to keep track. The realization hits me hard—did I inadvertently let my birth control regimen slip through the cracks amidst the chaos of my schedule?

The thought of becoming a mother sends a cascade of questions tumbling through my mind. Can I really take on such a monumental responsibility? The idea of it all makes my head spin—purchasing diapers and baby formula, navigating preschool and the entirety of K through 12 education, not to mention imparting general wisdom to a new human being. How are parents equipped to do all of that? That task seems almost insurmountable, particularly since my own parents were so damn good at it. Given how overstretched I am, how could I possibly muster the parenting skills necessary, especially when I've been so preoccupied that I've lost track of my own birth control schedule?

"I'm screwed," I mutter under my breath, the car coming to a stop in front of the drugstore.

Exhaling deeply, I lean back against the driver's seat, allowing myself a moment to consider any possible positives. There's one undeniable bright spot: my parents. They would be incredible grandparents, always willing and eager to lend a helping hand. This thought alone offers a sliver of comfort amidst the storm of anxieties swirling within me.

The realization that I might actually be capable of handling motherhood begins to dawn on me.

After all, I consider myself a good person, someone who generally gets along well with others. It stands to reason that my own child would have no reason not to like me. And when it comes to the baby's father, Randy, there's a lot to be optimistic about. His culinary skills alone speak volumes about his capability and dedication. The Calypso Café has managed to keep his menu alive in his absence, but it's clear to everyone, customers included, that Randy's unique touch is sorely missed. The food remains good, yet there's a unanimous agreement that it just isn't the same without him. He has the touch, and in more ways than one.

The thought of pregnancy brings me to the realization that Randy needs to know. It's true that he hasn't been in touch, but there's likely a good reason. Perhaps the constraints of being on a competitive cooking show have something to do with it.

"Yeah," I say softly to myself, comforted by this rationalization. That must be why Randy hasn't called. It's a small consolation, but it eases my mind as I prepare to face whatever comes next.

Taking a deep, calming breath, I muster the courage to step out of my car. Before I know it, I'm walking beneath the bright, fluorescent lights of the drugstore. My mind is in a haze as I navigate the aisles, eventually finding my way to the section where pregnancy tests are stocked. A sudden surge of optimism hits me—the idea of being pregnant seems ludicrous now. I'm probably just overworked, and my delayed period is merely my body's way of urging me to slow down and reprioritize my life.

With a newfound sense of confidence, I reach for the most popular brand of pregnancy test on the shelf. Holding it in my hand, I make my way to the checkout counter. As I walk, I contemplate the future. By tomorrow, I'll need to decide which of my many responsibilities I'm willing to let go of. Perhaps it should be taking over Randy's role at the Calypso. While I've proven to myself that I'm capable of handling it, that doesn't necessarily mean I should continue to do so, especially at the expense of my own well-being.

I pay, avoiding the look of dread on the face of the woman who rings up my purchase. A woman, alone, buying a pregnancy test at this time of night—we both know what's going on here.

Back at home, I find myself in the bathroom, following the pregnancy test instructions that seem straightforward enough. Pee on the stick, wait three minutes, and then check the result. A pink plus sign means pregnant; a blue minus sign means not pregnant.

After using the test, I carefully place it on a clean paper towel on the bathroom counter and set a three-minute timer on my phone. The idea of watching Randy on TV is far from appealing right now; my nerves are too frayed for that. Instead, I try to empty my mind of any thoughts. A part of me wishes I could just toss the test into the waste-basket and pretend this night never happened.

Ding! The sound from my phone cuts through the silence, marking the end of my wait.

The twenty minutes feel like they vanished in an instant. I jump to my feet and rush toward the bath-room, halting just before the doorway to steady myself. This moment feels monumental. With a deep breath to steel my nerves, I step forward to face whatever awaits me on the counter. My eyes land on the result—a stark pink plus sign stares back at me.

"Shoot," I mutter under my breath. Frantically, I grab the box to double-check the instructions, hoping against hope I've made a mistake. But there's no error—pink unmistakably means pregnant.

Gazing into the mirror, I struggle to recognize the reflection staring back. My mind races, failing to grasp the reality of the situation. This result must be incorrect; perhaps the test is faulty. Convincing myself of a mistake, I decide to seek further confirmation.

Without a second thought, I dash out, driven by a need for certainty. Back at the drugstore, I select six more tests, choosing a variety of brands to eliminate any doubt. The cashier from my previous visit handles my purchase, her gaze laden with empathy. Yet I internally rebuff her silent pity. This can't be happening. I'm not ready to accept the possibility of pregnancy, so I cling to a sliver of hope that these tests will tell a different story.

Clutching the bag of tests tightly, I rush out into the cool night air, my mind racing as fast as my car. "It has to be a false positive," I say to myself, clinging to the notion as I speed toward my apartment. That first pink plus had to be a mistake.

Once home, I waste no time. In the bathroom, I line up the tests and begin the process anew, desperate for a different outcome. The first retest yields a blue cross, indicating positive. But wait… The lines are blurry, and that casts a shadow of doubt in my mind. Without pausing, I take another test, this time waiting only ten minutes before checking. Two double pink lines stare back at me—positive.

I can't stop; I move from one test to the next, each result echoing the first. My hope for a single negative result dwindles with every pink and blue cross and double pink lines that appear. My eyes blur with tears, and a headache throbs at my temples. Deep down, I know the truth, but I'm not ready to accept it. I'm searching for a miracle in the form of a negative test, clinging to the faintest sliver of hope amidst the growing certainty.

Hours seem to blur together as I find myself in the kitchen, mindlessly drinking water, trying to process everything. Four tests are complete, and I'm down to the last two. Despite feeling like I've emptied myself completely, I manage to muster just enough urine for the final attempts. Back in the bathroom, I use the remaining tests, and this time, the results are swift and undeniable. Both display the pink plus sign within minutes, sealing my fate and leaving little to no room for doubt.

Resigned, I arrange all seven tests on the

counter, their unanimous verdict impossible to ignore. They seem to speak to me, a chorus of inanimate objects delivering the most life-altering news. "Wake up, you fool," they seem to say. "The baby's on its way, but you've got this. Don't worry, Gina. You'll be just fine."

CHAPTER 14

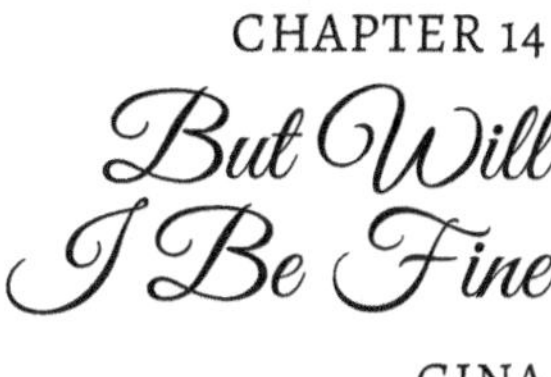

But Will I Be Fine

GINA

"Oh my God, Nom, what should I do?" The words spill out in a flood of fear and confusion. My world feels like it's in free fall. After sobbing into a pillow, demolishing a half-carton of banana nut white chocolate ice cream, and more tears, I found myself sprawled on the living room floor. It was only when the realization of my pregnancy hit me again that I reached out to Naomi.

The moment she answered the phone, I told her the truth: "I'm pregnant!"

Her response was swift and filled with concern: "I'll be there soon."

True to her word, Naomi arrived in just seventeen minutes. As she stepped into my apartment, the weight of my situation momentarily lifted as we hugged each other tightly. Her warm and reassuring presence anchors me amid my chaotic emotions.

"Gosh, Gina," she whispers, offering comfort with a gentle rub on my back. "Let's go sit."

I nod, and together, we head to the sofa. As I sink into the cushions' comforting embrace, I admit, "I still don't know what to do."

Naomi looks at me with such kindness. "Do you want to keep the baby?" she gently asks, her tone letting me know I have her support no matter what I decide.

"Yes," I reply without hesitation. During my earlier turmoil of emotions and the ice cream binge, I realized I wanted to hold on to the blossoming life inside me. Yet there's a significant concern I can't ignore. "It's Randy," I confess. "I don't know what he wants."

"So we're confirming that Randy is the father?" Naomi probes gently.

I look down and nod slightly, feeling a bit embarrassed because the last time we discussed it, I adamantly denied the possibility of Randy being the father.

"It's okay, Gina," Naomi reassures me, her voice soothing. "Everything is peachy keen."

I raise my head, and slowly, we begin to smile at

each other. I love her so dearly. Naomi Sutters is truly the best friend anyone could ask for. I struck gold back in the third grade when the cute little girl with a chipped front tooth visited my father's dental office for a repair. Our bond formed instantly. While I was busy with my homework, she approached and sat next to me, offering help because she loved schoolwork.

Together, we breezed through my math homework, proving even then that we were a great team. "I love math," she had said, "because I love logic."

"Logic?" I had asked, curious.

She then took the time to explain what logic was. I was amazed, not just by her intelligence, but by how fun she was too. After finishing the homework and with time to spare before her appointment, we played with the sit-down table tennis set in the waiting room.

When it was her turn in my dad's chair, Naomi suddenly looked a bit scared. Her dad was at work. He would return to pick her up later but couldn't stay with her for the appointment. Feeling alone, she asked if I could stay in the room with her, and my dad agreed. We spent that dental session bombarding my dad with all sorts of silly questions.

"Can a frog have two heads?" Naomi asked, her

words muffled because the mouth prop held her mouth open.

"Sometimes three," my dad joked.

We both broke out in laughter, knowing my dad gave us a silly answer to her silly question. From that day forward, we were inseparable. But who could have ever predicted that years later we would be here, side by side, coming to terms with my accidental pregnancy?

Naomi and I still sit in silence, but I feel compelled to express my greatest concern about telling Randy the news.

"I'm so rooted in this small town," I begin hesitantly. "And Randy… well, he's accustomed to the big city life. I don't want to make him feel like he has to give up his dreams because of this situation."

Naomi's thoughtful "hmm" fills the silence as she contemplates her next words. It's one of the many things I cherish about her; she never rushes to judgment or advice, making her destined to be an outstanding lawyer.

"Do you have any idea how far along you are?" she finally asks.

The question sends my mind spiraling back to that unforgettable night with Randy, a memory that now seems shrouded in a dream-like haze. Despite the clarity of that night fading, the significance of it doesn't.

"I'm not sure," I reply, although deep down, I know that's not entirely true. Before that night, Randy and I were all about urgency and fiery passion. But that night was different; it was as if we allowed ourselves to truly feel, to savor each other in a way we never had before. I feel like if destiny had a moment, it had to have been then.

Naomi probes further. "And you haven't spoken to him since he left?"

Curled up on my sofa, I wrap my arms around my knees, seeking solace in the small comfort it provides. "No," I admit with a heavy heart.

Naomi mirrors my sadness with a sympathetic downturn of her lips. Then she quickly changes her expression to ask, "Did you catch tonight's episode of *Head Chef Total Domination*?"

I shake my head and then gesture toward the TV. "He's in there, though," I say. "He's in my DVR."

"Okay then." Naomi reaches for the remote. "Let's watch Randy. Maybe seeing him will remind you that you're going to be okay."

Her suggestion sparks hope within me, yet I

pause, reaching out to gently touch her leg. "Wait just a moment."

Naomi halts as she looks at me, waiting for me to speak.

Resolved to reveal the truth, especially now that my unexpected pregnancy has left me with little to lose, I recount to Naomi the entirety of my last night with Randy. I share the depth of our connection, my hopeful anticipation for a blossoming relationship, and the unfortunate timing of missing his crucial phone call the next day. I tell her that he promised to call me back when he could, but that call never came.

"And you couldn't get in touch with him?" Naomi asks, her expression intensely curious.

I can only respond with a shake of my head, feeling the weight of missed opportunities.

Naomi's lips twist as she considers the possibilities. "Maybe he's on a closed set," she muses.

"What's a closed set?" My knowledge of TV production lingo is scant, having only recently dipped my toes into the world through my segment on my parents' podcast.

She explains the restrictions often placed on communication to and from contestants on shows to prevent spoilers or influence. "The show doesn't want to risk any leaks," she elaborates.

Her explanation makes me hopeful that Randy isn't just ignoring me because he's put me and our town in his rearview mirror. With my newfound optimism, I grasp onto that possibility.

"That has to be it," I claim, allowing myself a genuine smile for the first time in what feels like an eternity.

"I think that's a promising assumption to make," Naomi says, smiling along with me. "And Gina?"

I perk up. "Yes?"

She leans in, the air thick with anticipation. "You could've told me, you know."

I nod, feeling a bit sheepish. "I know. Keeping it to myself was more about me than you. I've never been in love before."

Naomi's eyes widen, a mix of surprise and delight on her face. "Ooh, love? That's a word I've never heard you use about anyone."

I laugh and give her knee a playful tap. "Just play the episode already."

After a few clicks on the remote, the screen comes to life with the opening scenes of *Head Chef*

Total Domination pulling us into the excitement of the competition.

As the show begins, the judges are introduced one by one. There are three of them, with Chef Robbie Price taking the lead. He sets the stage by telling the audience that they're about to witness some of the world's finest chefs in action. My excitement skyrockets when Chef Randy Thorn is the first to be introduced. With a confident curl of his arm and a flex of his muscles, he positions himself as the chef to watch.

Naomi glances at me, her eyebrows arched in admiration. "He's so hot."

I can't help but agree. "Very hot."

Our attention is riveted to the screen as the next two chefs are announced. The suspense for the culinary battle to begin is nail-biting.

Then comes the moment that turns my world on its head as the next introduction is made. "Chef Deanna Blume, Food and Spirits Chef of the Year, renowned for her elevated American cuisine," the announcer says.

My reaction is visceral. My neck cranes forward, and my jaw slackens. "That's her," I manage to whisper, disbelief coloring my tone. "The woman from the pier that night. He told me she was his manager, but what is she doing competing on a cooking show?" I turn to Naomi, searching for an explanation in her eyes, but she's just as taken aback as I am.

She gestures at the TV. "Let's just watch and see what happens. I mean, just because she's his manager doesn't mean she isn't a chef."

"I don't understand why he didn't mention that they were competing in the same competition," I say as more contestants are introduced.

"It *is* odd," Naomi concurs.

The tension in the air thickens as the show goes on. Watching is no fun at all. Deanna's always standing near him except when they're cooking. Watching Randy chop, dice, mix, and put his dish together is a lesson in pure mastery. When he tastes his food, adjusting here and there, it's clear he's in his zone.

Finally, time's up. The judges taste his entrée. Guest chef judge Jack Lay, a titan in the culinary world, praises Randy after sampling his dish. "Good to have you back."

After he says that, a video of Randy's backstory is played. Mentored by one of the greatest chefs in the world, Randy worked in one of the most famous kitchens in New York City until addiction brought a halt to his rising star. But he's recovered now and living in the small town where he was born. And according to Chef Jack Lay, he is better than ever, which is perhaps why Randy eventually wins the first competition of the episode.

"How are you doing?" Naomi asks, her eyebrows raised in concern as she checks in.

I nod stiffly. I'm managing okay until the show begins to drop hints about Deanna and Randy's past relationship. Other contestants express their surprise; one even comments on how beautiful their babies would be. Then when Randy wins the final cooking challenge of the episode. Deanna's excitement is explosive. She jumps into his arms, and Randy, in turn, lifts her and spins her around.

"Turn it off," I demand, unable to reach the remote control myself.

Without hesitation, Naomi complies.

"Oh my God," she exclaims, clearly as shocked and perhaps as disappointed as I am.

We sit there in stunned silence.

"You know, Gina, there has to be an explanation," Naomi says after a pause. "Especially after what you told me about your final night together."

"I know you're trying to help," I manage to say, attempting to fend off the onslaught of negative thoughts clouding my mind. Someone once said that our minds aren't engineered for happiness; they're built for survival. And right now, my mind is in full survival mode, painting scenarios where Randy seduced me that final night, fully aware of my turmoil at seeing him with another woman. It suggests that he wanted one last night with me, achieved his goal, and now there's more at stake with my pregnancy while he seemingly falls for someone else.

Or worse, was he in love with her all along? If I'm smart, I would protect my heart from him. I would start the process of getting over him five minutes ago.

THE NEXT DAY

Naomi offered to stay the night, but I encouraged her to go home and be with Derek. This morning, I felt utterly run-down, as if I'd been steamrolled in my sleep. Yet knowing the reason behind my morning nausea didn't make it any easier to deal with. Thankfully, a quick online search gave me some remedies for morning sickness. I found I had peppermint tea in the cabinet and a good amount of fresh ginger root in the refrigerator. Mixing them into lukewarm water and drinking the liquid slowly helped ease my nausea significantly.

Next, I reluctantly made the call I'd been dreading—I called my doctor. I explained my situation to the medical receptionist, telling her about the multiple pregnancy tests and my missed period. I was surprised when she offered me an appointment for ten o'clock this morning due to a last-minute cancellation. I took it. It was a stroke of luck, being that I have no classes today and I'm not due at Calypso until noon.

So now I'm here, wearing only a thin cloth gown, while sitting on my OBGYN's examination table. It has been nearly a year since I've had an appointment directly with Dr. Haskell. When I come in for birth control injections, I'm tended to by a nurse practitioner. But I've been a patient of Dr. Haskell's for as long as I can remember. She's seen me through some very pivotal moments of my life. Like my first period. Before heading off to university my mom made me an appointment, aiming to arm me with knowledge of safe sex practices and birth control. I remember Dr. Haskell as being unwaveringly pragmatic yet incredibly delicate in her approach, which remains unchanged.

I already took another pregnancy test, this time in a clinical setting, followed by a series of blood tests. While waiting for my results and further examination, I find myself with so much downtime that I actually close my eyes and rest on the examination table.

My mind is crowded with thoughts, with Randy occupying a significant portion. I've always made an effort not to be one of those individuals whose happiness is significantly affected by their romantic relationships. Yet here I am, caught in the emotional turmoil Randy has unwittingly caused.

I clench eyes more tightly shut. "Focus, Gina," I tell myself, trying desperately to redirect my thoughts away from him.

One day, I might actually become a mother. Perhaps, I'm not entirely certain yet. There's a chance something I consumed yesterday could've skewed all my tests toward false positives.

"Let's just think this through," I whisper to the silent room, seeking solace in my own voice amidst the uncertainty.

The sound of the door gently creaking interrupts my thoughts, and I open my eyes to see Dr.

Haskell entering the room. She's always impeccably dressed, her appearance as precise and polished as ever. Complemented by flawlessly applied makeup, her neat bob haircut has always reminded me of Anna Wintour. Dr. Haskell smiles, her movements gentle and measured as she gracefully takes a seat in her black leather chair, her gaze fixed on me with an unwavering intensity.

"Yes, you are indeed pregnant," she states unequivocally, cutting through the fog of my doubts and theories about potential false positives that I hastily shared at the start of my appointment.

My mouth opens, but no words come out. Dr. Haskell, however, continues with the practicalities, informing me that we will proceed with an ultrasound to determine how far along I am. Plus, she will be prescribing prenatal vitamins. As she speaks, I try my best to absorb her instructions, nodding along as she emphasizes the importance of regular, low-impact exercise for both my well-being and the baby's. She hands me a pamphlet detailing beneficial exercises, recommending yoga for its benefits in enhancing breathing, endurance, and flexibility.

When we're done, she says I should stop at the front desk before leaving her office to schedule my next three appointments. The frequency of our meetings will increase as my pregnancy progresses. For the initial seven months, I'm to see her once every four weeks, shifting to weekly visits thereafter.

The reality of the situation sinks in with each word spoken. The thought of my body changing so drastically over the next several months is almost surreal.

"So… a whole baby is actually going to come out of me?" I blurt out, a bit overwhelmed by the thought.

Dr. Haskell pauses, giving me a look that seems to acknowledge my anxiety for the first time. "Yes, darling, that's exactly what will happen," she assures me gently. "But remember, I'll be with you every step of the way until you're holding your beautiful child in your arms. I'm one of the best in this field, and I promise to do everything within my power to reduce your pain and ensure your comfort. You're stronger than you think, and you'll get through this beautifully."

Wow, I believe her. That's the beauty of having an OBGYN with her demeanor and thoroughness. I'm also surprised that she didn't ask about the baby's father, and I feel compelled to share. "His name is Randy," I say, feeling a bit exposed. "And he doesn't know yet."

Dr. Haskell's expression remains calm and professional. "Gina, I want you to know I'm not here to judge you. My role is to support you through this journey, no matter your situation."

Nodding, I feel a wave of relief wash over me.

"Now," Dr. Haskell says, her small smile lighting up her usually inexpressive face, "let's find out how far along you are."

---

15 MINUTES LATER

Feeling detached from my body, as if this moment belongs to someone else, I watch Dr. Haskell maneuver the ultrasound stick inside me. But the words she has just uttered seem impossible to grasp.

"Eight weeks?" I echo, squinting from disbelief and the instrument up my vagina. "No, that can't be right. No." My head vehemently shakes in denial.

"Yes," she affirms, her voice a pillar of calm certainty as she finally takes that thing out of me.

The realization dawns on me, leaving my thoughts in disarray. Doing the math feels beyond me. The last time Randy and I were together was magical, the kind of moment you might one day recount to your grown children when they ask about their beginnings. But the thought of explaining to my child that their life started during a midnight bang on the kitchen counter at Calypso Café is too much to bear.

"Gina?" Dr. Haskell's voice reaches me again, and this time, I feel her hand gripping mine. "Goodness, darling, you need to find your calm. I'm prescribing a specific exercise regime for you. Yoga, three times a week. Frannie will give you the details for a studio you can attend. All my patients get a 50 percent discount on their monthly membership. Did you catch all that, or do you need me to go over it again?"

Her tone demands a response, so I quickly reply, "I understand."

I call into the Calypso and inform Sarah that I won't be able to make it in today.

"Are you okay?" she asks. "You sound terrible."

Summoning all my strength, I reply, "I'm fine."

The news I received during the ultrasound still rattles me for some inexplicable reason. I hardly recognize myself anymore. I need a few days to find my way back to who I used to be. Fortunately, I'm not due back at the Calypso until Monday.

Now, with no obligations looming over me, I'm curled up in bed, exhausted but too restless to sleep. Rolling onto my back, I find myself staring aimlessly at that spot on the ceiling above my bed. I really should do something about it. Perhaps I'll paint over it or install a ceiling fan. I should do something about how I feel too. Maybe some meditation and a healthier diet will help. Less stress about Randy would help too. I need to mature quickly and prepare to be the mother our child deserves.

CHAPTER 15

Podcast With Parents

GINA

Two weeks after finding out I'm pregnant, things are surprisingly smooth. I've decided to tackle life one breath at a time whenever I can. Yoga has been a lifesaver in that regard, teaching me to breathe through any situation that prevents me from tumbling into the depths of despair.

I've steered clear of watching any more episodes of *Head Chef Total Domination*. Everyone, including my parents, seems engrossed in the show, wildly cheering on our hometown hero. Rumors about Randy and Deanna's on-screen chemistry have reached me, but Sarah and Rita assure me it's all for show.

"That's not how he behaves when he's truly

interested in someone," Sarah insists whenever talk of my former lover and the father of my child surfaces. I deflect these conversations as best I can, yet I can't help but picture him captivating viewers on their screens with his intense expression during competitions or when he lights up with joy after each victory. He has been practically unbeatable.

"And… action!" my dad interjects, snapping me back to reality.

It's Thursday, which means it's time for my segment on the podcast. The camera is rolling, ready to capture me. I'm positioned at an outdoor kitchen setup that my dad has constructed specifically for these shows. With the spotlight on, I flash a wide, genuinely happy smile, ready to engage my audience.

"Today, we're diving into a new baking adventure—rosemary and blackberry scones filled with creamy ricotta." I gesture toward the vibrant group of women who've known me all my life. They're the heart of our podcast, the empty nesters who lunch, notorious for their candid chats about their kids. I've miraculously stayed off their radar, but as life throws its curveballs, I wonder how long that will last.

"For a twist," I continue. "Our mystery ingredient is..."

The ladies exchange looks, their excitement bubbling over. "Cayenne!" they announce in unison, throwing me a culinary curveball.

"Okay," I sing, accepting the challenge. My mind is already racing with possibilities. How to incorporate the fiery heat of cayenne into the delicate sweetness of the scones?

Linda eyes me with a mix of curiosity and a dare. "Is that enough of a challenge for you?"

It's my job to smile at her question. My performance as the cheerful yet capable dessert chef has been impeccable thus far. That's why podcast listeners and viewers love me. "Absolutely!" I exclaim. "It's all about balancing the unexpected."

"But she's always up for it," Carrie remarks with a knowing wink. "Who could forget her vanilla bean and lavender sweet potato croquettes?"

My mom theatrically clasps her hand over her heart while stretching out her other hand to give Carrie's shoulder a gentle squeeze. "Indeed, Carrie, they were a hit, and they sold out way too fast. But hey, she's my daughter. So guess how I convinced her to make more of those treats for the woman who endured thirteen hours of labor bringing her into the world?"

Joyce gasps exaggeratedly. "No? You played the birth card?"

Carrie raises a finger for emphasis. "I too would play the birth card for a batch of those croquettes."

With a megawatt smile directed at the camera, Nori wraps up. "And remember, the scrumptious dessert that's whipped up by our brilliant chef today will be ready and waiting for you to buy at The Calypso Café come Monday morning. You already know you should get there early because they never last long!"

"Everything she makes is mouthwatering," my mom boasts.

"Are you bragging, Faye?" Joyce teases, her voice laced with amusement.

With a playful shrug, my mom replies, "What can I say? My daughter is perfect. She didn't even hurt my…" My mom's whistle sounds like 'woo-hoo'… "when she came out after that fifteen hours of labor." My mom's tone is comedic.

"You said thirteen hours, Faye," Linda, another cohost, teases.

"Thirteen, fifteen, what's the difference? Who

am I kidding? She stretched me to kingdom come, that one."

All the ladies laugh except for Joyce, who emits a playful huff before declaring, "Well, I'm beginning to doubt I have the perfect son."

And now, it officially starts, which is why I lower my gaze. I want to make sure I don't get dragged into the burgeoning gossip fest.

Everyone in my class who attended Roosevelt High remembers Mike Nelson, Joyce's son. He wasn't the star of the school, but somehow, he was everywhere. He was standing with the photography club at assemblies. He's still memorialized in the hallways in a photo of the chess club from the year they won the state championship. I used to see him climb on a bus with the debate team to go to competitions. Once, he was honored by our principal for organizing a successful food drive. He nearly snagged the title of class valedictorian. Mike was also in the band, a benchwarmer for the varsity basketball team, and even took part in the drama club. Mike was a do, do, doer. Now that I know Joyce much better, I understand why.

The latest on Mike is that he left his software programming gig in Silicon Valley. "He's joined a band," Joyce reveals with a hint of disapproval. "In New York City, no less."

The other ladies express their surprise, my mom included, which catches me off guard. After all, she has been through her own dramatic career changes, just like me.

"From making twenty-five thousand dollars a month to joining a garage band?" Carrie's disbelief is obvious, as if Mike's decision defies all reason.

"She never specifically said it was a garage band," my mom interjects, her comment marking a return to her more rational self. "What kind of band is it, Joyce?"

"I don't care what kind of band it is. It's still a band, not a real job," Joyce retorts, clearly frustrated.

Turning to me, Nori inquires, "What do you think, Gina?"

At that moment, I realize I had stopped working to stare at them. *Dang it!* I didn't mean to seem like I was paying attention. They've done this before, asked me to comment on gossip about one of my peers. Usually, I say something like, "I think you should change the subject." They laugh and then move on to the next kid.

But this time, I don't want to do that, especially

now that I'm expecting a child of my own. "Bravo for him because he's finally choosing to do something for himself." I hold back from adding "and not you" out of respect for my elders, as my parents taught me.

"Well, he graduated from MIT," Joyce fires back.

I'm left speechless, my cheeks warming. Honestly, I couldn't care less if Mike is in a garage band or has joined the greatest band in the world. I really want to tell her to stop dragging me into their gossip. I'm baffled that none of their children have issued them a cease and desist yet.

"That was a good point, Gina," my mom finally says, giving me an out, for which I'm immensely grateful.

Joyce, lips pursed in a pout, clearly doesn't share the sentiment.

"Anyway, speaking of local talent, what about *Head Chef Total Domination*?" Linda interjects.

Ugh. Great. I mentally roll my eyes. They've segued from one uncomfortable topic to another.

"Randy Thorn is dominating the competition," Carrie announces with pride.

Comments bounce among them, touching on Randy's tragic family history. They mention the terrible car accident that took his parents' lives and how proud they would be of him now. Some reminisce about Blair Thorn, Randy's mother. They remember her as likable and an avid swimmer at the community center in Bradley Ridge. They agree that Randy strongly resembles his father, Jeff Thorn.

"He was so handsome," they say, except for my mom and Linda, who moved to town after the Thorns' tragic accident and didn't know them.

A moment of commemorative silence lingers.

"Well, his handsome son has been making me fat with all that butter in his delicious food," my mom says, moving the conversation into a lighter place.

"Oh, Chef Randy's food is to die for," Joyce replies, her mood lightening from the earlier topic of Mike.

"He's definitely going to win," Carrie asserts, swirling her drink in her glass. I had almost overlooked their midday cocktail indulgence. "After he wins, I doubt he'll ever come back." She turns to my mom. "That means no more butter for you, Faye."

The ladies laugh as those words hit me like a ton of bricks, making me freeze on the spot.

"But Gina has been covering for him in the kitchen, and she's doing an incredible job," my mom proudly declares.

Heat floods my cheeks at the mention of my name in the same breath as Randy's, stirring a mix of pride and anxiety within me.

"I'm sure he'll return to town when the show is over," Joyce asserts. "I've spoken with him plenty of times. Chef Randy is very happy here."

I almost reach out to my dad through the microphone in my earpiece, wanting him to shift the cameras from the gossiping group back to me. I'm eager to steer the conversation away from Randy and share my culinary plans for the cayenne pepper challenge with the audience.

However, Linda's next comment stops me. She muses that Deanna Blume might whisk Randy away to the kind of upscale dining scenes far removed from our simple-town life, someplace where elaborate ten-course meals are the norm.

I lower my head once more, struggling against the urge to hyperventilate. For some reason, I'm teetering on the edge of losing control.

"No..." My mom interjects gently. "First, he has to come home. If he wins—"

"You mean *when* he wins," Joyce confidently corrects her.

"Yes, when he wins," my mom agrees. "Mayor Salley will surely organize a parade in his honor."

"Right down Main Street," someone adds, though in my flustered state, I can't tell who.

"And since he and Gina are friends," my mom continues, "perhaps she could persuade him to join us here at our table when he returns."

Focused on the task at hand, I feel their eyes lingering on me, but I steadfastly avoid meeting their gazes. Their recent words about Randy and Deanna have left me shaken, making it impossible for me to discuss him right now. Ignoring their attempts to engage me, I pivot, lower myself, and begin plucking mint for my mom's petite garden.

Abruptly, my dad's alarmed voice crackles through my earpiece. "What's going on, Love Bug?"

"I'm baking," I manage to utter, my voice betraying my attempt at stability.

"Did you even hear the question?" he asks urgently.

I spring to my feet, but the sudden movement sends my head spinning. The world swirls around me uncontrollably.

"Could someone please fetch our baker a drink?" a voice calls out.

But I can't have a cocktail.

"She seems a bit tense today," another voice remarks.

Perhaps I am tense today.

My gaze settles on the women at the table. They haven't let the matter go; they're still watching me, waiting for my response. Little do they know they're poking a hornet's nest. If I keep reacting like this, they'll start suspecting there's more to it. In fact, I'm the juiciest gossip they don't even know they're staring at. So I have to keep it together. I force a smile, summoning one that could rival any game show hostess's.

"Oh, absolutely! Randy Thorn is an incredible chef," I exclaim with feigned enthusiasm. Then I fabricate, "My top priority will be to get him on your show if he returns to us. But before we get into that, let me share what I have in mind for this!" I proudly display a large handful of mint.

All eyes shift to my hand, prompting me to take a closer look as well. Goodness gracious. I've inadvertently uprooted the entire plant. Yet I maintain composure and smoothly transition into detailing my plans for a mint, blackberry, and cayenne drizzle to elevate the flavors of my scones.

Joyce stifles a yawn, while Linda hurriedly glances at her phone. The only person who seems genuinely engaged, rather than glazed over in boredom as I detail my baking process, is my mom. The other ladies always seem uninterested in the baking portion, preferring to get straight to the tasting. Nevertheless, I've successfully shifted the conversation away from Randy. Five minutes later, when I hand the spotlight back to them, they move to a new topic, discussing the expenses and efforts involved in transforming their children's former bedrooms into hobby rooms. As Joyce puts it, "After Mike left, I needed a hobby."

I'm pretty sure she did.

The empty nesters who lunch have departed, slightly tipsy and patting themselves on the back from all the comments by fans gushing about today's show. The hosts will be back on Tuesday, but thankfully, my segment is only once a week. It was brutal for me today. Of course I've participated in their discussions in the past, but this is the first time I had something to hide.

I'd rather go straight home to avoid my parents, who are looking at me as if they suspect something is off, but I have a whole boatload of laundry to finish. I think I've reached the point in life where I should search for a bigger place to live, one with a washer and dryer, an en suite bathroom, at least two bedrooms, and a backyard. I must prepare my life to comfortably accept a child who will be here in almost seven months.

"Hey, you," my mom says, poking her head into the laundry room.

Her sudden appearance makes me jump. "Hey," I reply.

She steps in and kisses me on the temple. "Sorry to startle you."

"It's fine," I manage to say, fighting back a surge of emotions stirred by her kiss and tone of voice.

Dressed in a blue and white Raglan T-shirt and faded jeans, my mom leans against the cabinets, crossing her arms. She always changes into something more comfortable after the show. Now she exudes a casual and relaxed vibe as she asks, "Are you not feeling well today?"

The dryer's buzz signals the completion of my

final load. In that moment, I ponder how much easier it might be to just tell my mom I'm pregnant. However, considering her agreement with the others about the chemistry between Randy and Deanna at the table today, it doesn't seem like the right time. I think it's better to wait until Randy's show isn't the main topic of conversation in town.

With a forced smile, I open the dryer door and assure her. "I feel A-okay, Mom."

Her gaze lingers on me, as if she's trying to read between the lines of my feigned composure.

"You know you can come to me with anything," she offers, her maternal instinct likely in overdrive.

"I know," I respond, transferring the warm laundry onto the folding table.

"I apologize for the unexpected detour into the world of Chef Thorn and Deanna Blume. I couldn't help but notice a certain spark between you two. Has that been sorted out?"

Her question catches me off guard, leaving my mouth hanging open in disbelief. With her expectant raised eyebrows, it's clear she doesn't miss much.

Now I find myself needing to steer the conversation in a different direction, and fast. "Randy and I are simply friends," I blurt out, though thoughts of my impending motherhood linger in the back of my mind. Technically, it's not a lie. If we're to navigate co-parenting in the future, friendship would certainly be beneficial. "But let's talk about Mike Nelson."

My tactic seems to work, as she raises her head slightly, indicating that I've successfully diverted her attention from Randy.

"Mom, you've always encouraged me to explore new avenues, to be bold in pursuit of happiness," I say, hoping to sway her. "You know Mike and the others could really use your support, especially with their own mothers. Joyce was particularly tough on him today."

My mom furrows her eyebrows, considering my plea.

Now that I've got her attention, I press on, seizing the moment. "What they said about Lacy's boyfriend last week wasn't kind either. Few people my age have it all figured out these days, including myself. When my time comes, how will you react?"

Her expression shifts suddenly, and a hint of concern flickers in her eyes. Perhaps I've revealed too much.

"So there is something you're not telling me?" she probes.

I shake my head emphatically. "No, I'm just making a point."

Mom grunts thoughtfully, lost in contemplation once more. "I was supposed to be the comic relief, but it seems I've become the voice of reason instead," she remarks with a laugh tinged with irony. "But you're right, Love Bug. I'll speak up from now on."

"Great," I say, feeling a wave of relief wash over me, knowing that sooner rather than later, I'll likely find myself on the chopping block of the lunching empty nesters.

CHAPTER 16

Calypso Collapse

GINA

It's Monday morning, and the line at the Calypso is out the door. Customers are clamoring for my rosemary and blackberry scones filled with creamy ricotta. I came in at 3 a.m. to start baking, just after Pete leaves and a full two hours before Kai arrives, to ensure everything is ready. Planning for high demand, I made five hundred scones, setting a limit of three per customer at $8.99 each, hoping to accommodate everyone. Yet they sell out within an hour.

Having purchased all the ingredients myself, I retain 75 percent of the profits, which means I've made $3,371.25 this morning alone. It's a little less after deducting the cost of ingredients. Ever since the podcast took off, Mondays have become incredibly profitable.

"You made a lot of money this morning," Sarah comments, clearly happy about my earnings.

"I know," I reply with a happy yawn, struggling to keep standing after waking up at 2:30 a.m. I really should get some rest because I have to be back again at 1 p.m. to get ready for the dinner shift.

"I'll input your sales into the system and get you paid before..." Sarah's voice trails off as her attention snaps to something—or someone—who is just walking into the café.

It's Steve, who usually doesn't come in this early. He's scowling as usual. His clothes are crumpled, face unshaven, and eyes are blood red. Basically, he looks as if he hasn't showered in weeks.

"What is he doing here?" I murmur, barely moving my lips.

"Oh my God, he's a train wreck," Sarah whispers back.

It hardly matters if he notices us staring and whispering about him because Steve's attention is riveted on the sizable crowd who has lingered for breakfast and coffee after missing out on the scones.

"He's probably seeing headcount as dollar signs," Sarah mutters under her breath.

Steve's glassy eyes skip right past me and zero in on Sarah. "Sarah, I need to speak with you in my office," he says and continues on his way.

Watching him, Sarah's expression turns grim, as if she's witnessing a disaster unfold. She squeezes my arm tightly. "Damn it. I'll make sure you get paid for your podcast pastries this morning," she assures me.

I manage a small nod, concealing my surprise. I had believed that the days when Steve nearly ran this place into the ground were behind us, especially with Jeremy stepping in as his reliable caretaker. It seems, however, that I might have assumed too much.

I can't have any delay in the funds owed to me. I desperately need the money I made this morning. On Saturday, I went hunting for a new place to live and found a charming cottage with a sprawling, grassy backyard right by a lake. I planned to use today's earnings as a security deposit.

Too exhausted to linger long enough to learn the outcome of Sarah's meeting with Steve, I have no choice but to leave. On my way home, I feel a wave of relief wash over me as an electronic notification from my bank pings on my phone—the funds have been deposited. Now I can rest easy.

When I get home, I head straight to bed. Upon waking, life resumes its familiar pace. As the days unfold, my pregnancy sometimes feels almost imperceptible, likely because I stay diligently hydrated. Determined not to stress my body unnecessarily, I have also begun reading books on maintaining a healthy and happy pregnancy. I'm grateful that Dr. Haskell encouraged me to start yoga; the combination of breath and movement has significantly improved my mental health.

These days, thoughts of Randy rarely cross my mind, even when Pete comes into the bakery full of enthusiasm, often boasting about Randy's latest dominating performance on the show. "He's going to win it all. He's unbeatable," Pete declares now and then.

I find it easier to listen to Pete's updates because he never mentions Deanna. For that, I am grateful.

On Thursday afternoon, after wrapping up my segment on the podcast, I find myself with a few hours to spare before I need to hit the road for Naomi's law school graduation. It's a bittersweet moment because I know it could have been both of us celebrating if I hadn't dropped out. I can't help but wonder: What if I had persevered? I remember slogging through legal briefs, so disinterested that the words seemed to blur into one another. If I had pushed through, would I have crossed paths with Randy? As I sit at my desk, looking down at my still-flat belly, where our child is growing, I ponder these what-ifs.

And yet amidst these reflections, I realize I haven't even told my parents about my pregnancy. Today's podcast episode was a tumultuous one too. Poor Javier was in the hot seat as Linda, his mother, publicly announced his looming divorce, declaring to everyone that he and his wife, Jessie, had married too young and that Jessie needed time to "figure herself out." Then, turning the spotlight on me unexpectedly, she asked, "Are you single, Gina?" That question, so pointed, still hangs in the air.

I wish I could have pretended not to hear her, but they've caught on to that trick by now. Instead of giving a direct answer, I met her inquiry with a stern glare, silently urging her to move on from that subject. No such luck.

"Are you?" she persisted.

Annoyed, I responded sharply, "Am I what, Linda?" I was exasperated by her insistence.

"Available, because you and Javi would make a good couple."

My jaw might as well have hit my prep table. Was she really trying to set me up with her son who's going through a divorce?

Thankfully, my mom came through on her promise to keep the empty nesters in check when they become overly critical of their children. With a tension-breaking joke, she said, "Okay, Linda, let her bake. We'll take the dowry when Javi's not still married. But for now, let's go around the table and say something positive about our offspring, starting with you, Joyce."

Without missing a beat and still in the posture she adopts when she's on the brink of saying something negative, Joyce chimed in. "Well, Mike promised he wouldn't need any money from me, ever. That's a positive."

Actually, that wasn't quite a positive. Nobody can make me appreciate my parents more than Joyce.

Despite the challenges, I still enjoy doing the show with the ladies. They can be a handful, but mostly, they are fun to be around.

Now, back at home and dressed for the graduation, I find myself with some spare time. Naturally, I start scrolling through my "Gina The Baker" Facebook account, where I've accumulated six thousand friends and followers who adore my baking. As I browse, my gaze drifts to the search bar. I recall that *Head Chef Total Domination*, the popular cooking show, has a Facebook page.

It wouldn't hurt to do a quick check-in, right? I briefly consider this before typing the show's name into the search bar. A few clicks later, I'm on their page, ready to see what's new.

But honestly, why does the first post have to be about Randy? As soon as I land on the page, there he is in the photo, his eyebrows drawn together in that intense focus he reserves for cooking. He's carefully pinching spices into a frying pan. The comments below the photo are predictable: some praise his handsome looks and culinary skills, while others criticize his stern demeanor.

"He's not nice," one woman comments bluntly. She's not entirely off the mark—Randy never pretends to be the friendliest person. But mean? Not exactly. Nitpicky? Definitely. A bit of a sourpuss? Sure. But when he smiles, it's like the sky splits open to sprinkle us with cherry lollipops.

The same woman also notes the lack of chemistry between Randy and his co-contestant Deanna, adding that she can't quite picture him having chemistry with anyone. I mean, this lady is extremely negative. It's obvious that she's not a happy camper. Yet she seems to be in the minority with her views on Randy and Deanna's dynamic.

"They're going to get together after this," another person boldly asserts, claiming to bet her life on it.

Meanwhile, one guy expresses his frustration with the current season, wishing they would drop all the fluff and return to the straightforward cooking format of past seasons.

Feeling queasy from the comments, I decide to take a break and make myself a lukewarm cup of fresh ginger tea with the ginger I grated earlier this morning. Once settled back at my computer, I decide I've had enough of reading the opinions of strangers, so I shift my focus to simply looking at photos of Randy. I miss him so much. Imagining a future without being by his side is daunting.

Deanna is incredibly lucky, and judging from photos of her, very pretty. Although it's challenging, I'm trying to recognize the positives in their relationship. After all, she knew him first. They were together before he ever met me. This situation has taught me a powerful lesson: sexual chemistry doesn't necessarily lay the foundation for a lasting relationship, no matter how electric it is. Apparently, successful relationships have that extra something Randy and I could never find together.

I stumble upon a post with a clickbait headline that reads, "Did you see that?" accompanied by the hashtag *#BunsOfSteel.* Curiosity gets the better of me, and I click to play the video. In it, Deanna walks past Randy and playfully slaps his tight bum. Randy responds with a playful finger wag and a snicker before he continues cooking. As I scroll through the comments, my throat tightens, each word feeling like it's choking me.

"They're a cute couple."

"I wonder how that tush felt against her hand."

"Do you see the way he looks at her?"

Then I read a comment that snaps me out of my scrolling frenzy. "How is that not sexual harassment?" I realize I've been clutching my stomach the entire time. Glancing at the top of the screen, I notice I'm late.

"Oh no!" I jump to my feet. Then I grab my keys and rush out of my apartment, more determined than ever to put emotional and mental distance between Randy and me. Lingering on these feelings just won't be healthy, especially as we navigate the complexities of co-parenting in the future.

It's Friday morning, and I'm relieved that the week is finally winding down. I got to the café early today after hearing that two of our three breakfast cooks were out sick, and Sarah was in a bind. With the flu making the rounds, Calypso Café strictly enforces a policy against coming to work ill. Despite desperately needing every extra minute of sleep, I couldn't say no when she asked me to help out. After all the support Sarah has given me, stepping in to assist her was the least I could do.

Pulling into the parking lot, I'm taken aback by the scene before me. The café opens in just over an hour, yet Sarah, Rita, and four other staff members are huddled in front of the door.

I quickly pull into the first available parking space and jump out of the car, my curiosity spiking. I hurry over to the group, anxious to find out what's wrong.

"What's going on?" I ask, trying to catch my breath as I approach them.

It doesn't take long to identify the issue, but Rita confirms it anyway. "The door is chained."

My jaw drops as we exchange looks of disbelief, all of us seemingly trapped in the same unexpected nightmare.

"Have you spoken to Steve yet?" I ask, my gaze fixed on Sarah, who is busy with her phone.

"I tried reaching him, but he's not answering," she explains. Lowering her voice, she adds, "Now I'm calling Jeremy." Holding the phone to her ear, she waits for him to pick up.

Rita, clearly furious, crosses her arms and shakes her head. "Well, he finally did it," she says bitterly. "Steve has been trying to run this place into the ground ever since I started working here, and now he's done it."

Carl, one of the cooks, looks worried. "So what does that mean? Do we go home without getting paid?"

Paul, another cook, chimes in. "That's right! It's payday."

Like everyone else, I feel a wave of panic. Although I haven't relied on a paycheck from Calypso for a while, thanks to my podcast gig, the thought of this place closing down hits hard. All of my friends are here; my social life revolves around this café. It's a third home to me, after my apartment and my parents' house.

Just then, Sarah's face changes as she hears a response on the phone. "Jeremy, there's a huge chain on every door," she says, her voice filled with a sigh of relief.

Sarah listens intently to Jeremy on the phone, her expression fluctuating between surprise and concern as he speaks. "Uh-huh," she repeats several times, her eyebrows darting up and down, mirroring the gravity of the conversation.

Suddenly, Jeremy says something that halts her midsentence, and all of us watch her closely, hanging on the silent communication. She nods slowly as if accepting and processing his words.

"The code is all eight digits of Steve's birthday and 3458," she finally responds. "Thank you so much, Jeremy. I'm sorry this happened too. I'll let everyone know."

She ends the call and turns to face us, ready to share the news. We are all anxious to hear what Jeremy has said about the situation.

CHAPTER 17

The End of An Era

GINA

We left the Calypso feeling slightly lighter, buoyed by Jeremy's assurances. He had promised that all employees would be paid by the end of the day. Just before Sarah called him, Jeremy had received a notification from the bank. Due to Steve's lack of response, the bank took ownership of Calypso Café at 6 a.m. to mitigate the risk of default. Since payroll was managed by an external company and all of Steve's accounts were either frozen or delinquent, Jeremy pledged to transfer sufficient funds to cover everyone's paycheck and add a month's severance.

"He's such a good guy," Sarah remarked, relief evident in her voice.

"And rich too," Rita added, bringing comic relief to the tense morning.

With our plans abruptly cleared and stomachs growling, Rita, Sarah, and I decided to go to the Golden Spoon for breakfast. The sensation of having no immediate responsibilities was unusual for me. I was no longer in school, and my only actual job, the podcast, hardly felt like one. Suddenly, I am starting to feel what it's like to live a stress-free life. It has been so long since my schedule allowed me to spend quality time with friends.

The soft chorus of laughter sparked by Rita's comment fades, and a reflective silence settles over us.

"I'm really going to miss you guys," Rita says, her fingers tracing the wood grain of the table, her voice tinged with melancholy.

"Same," Sarah agrees softly.

"Me too, a lot," I echo, feeling the weight of the moment. "So, what are you guys going to do?"

Rita lets out a heavy sigh that sounds like a deflating balloon. "I don't know. I guess I'll find another job."

Sarah begins to speak, hesitates, then sits up straighter, a spark of excitement lighting her eyes. She places a hand on her abdomen, and instantly, I understand the gesture. "Dan and I are pregnant," she announces, her voice brimming with joy.

"Ah!" Rita exclaims, clapping her hands together. "Congratulations!"

The joyous news jolts me, and I feel a pang of something bittersweet, like a withering rose amidst a blossoming garden. I gather my spirits, forcing myself to echo Rita's enthusiasm. "Yes, congratulations," I say with a smile. It truly is thrilling for Sarah, especially knowing how deeply Dan loves her. "I'm truly happy for you," I add sincerely, my heart swelling with joy for her despite my mixed emotions. I mean, it would be nice to announce news of my pregnancy. But that's just not an option right now.

Sarah's smile grows wider, and she seems to relax as she shares more about her life changes. "I think this is the universe working on my behalf, on all of our behalf really. Things were never going to end well as long as Steve owned the café. Working for him has been extremely nerve-wracking. He used the café like his own personal ATM, so I'm not shocked his practices finally caught up with him."

"I didn't know that," I admit, surprised by the revelation.

"It was stressful, too stressful," Sarah continues,

shaking her head as if to physically cast off the burden. "Dan and I have been discussing taking over his parents' apple orchard in Connecticut. I would run the business, and he would manage the mill."

"That sounds fun," I reply, feeling a twinge of sadness at the thought of not seeing Sarah as often.

"I'll miss you, though," Rita adds, her voice tinged with sadness. "But gosh, you're pregnant?" Rita asks, squeezing Sarah's arm affectionately. "How far along are you?"

"Two and a half months," she happily announces.

I stifle an urge to jump for joy. Sarah and I conceived around the same time. The thought of our children being born around the same date almost makes me want to share my news regardless of the scandal associated with my pregnancy. But still, I can't. I won't.

Suddenly, Rayna, the owner of the Golden Spoon, approaches our table, expertly balancing three plates of food. Her unexpected arrival instantly brightens our mood. Rayna wasn't the waitress who took our order, but her presence is as welcome as a ray of sunshine on a cloudy day. She's dressed casually in loose jeans rolled up above her ankles and a bright yellow T-shirt featuring a happy face print, starkly contrasting the typical attire of the Golden Spoon's waitstaff. After she places the plates on the table, we each rise to greet her with a warm hug.

Rayna, still standing at the edge of our table with her hands on her hips, frowns, obviously concerned. "Is it true that there's a chain on the door of the Calypso?" she asks.

We all nod, each chiming in with a quiet confirmation. As usual, news travels fast in this town.

"Wow," she murmurs, her gaze drifting off momentarily before she looks back at us. "Is Steve okay?"

"We don't know," Sarah replies, her voice low.

Rayna nods, her expression showing a mix of concern and understanding. Everyone in town is aware of Steve's gambling issues, and given her past with him, her concern is understandable. Rayna and Steve were an item before she married her current husband.

"Well, listen, if you're looking for another place to land, I would be happy to have you. Coming from the Calypso, you're the best crew in town."

We all exchange glances. Working together again, even in a different restaurant, is quite appealing.

"And Gina," Rayna says, her intense focus catching me off guard. "We know about your podcast and your Monday morning pastries. You're always sold out before I even get there. We've been thinking about expanding by adding a bakery. I would love to have you baking here."

I press my lips tightly together, contemplating her offer. It's certainly tempting. Yet the thought of working in a brand new kitchen—a space Randy has never occupied—fills my heart with sadness for a moment. But regardless, I say, "Thanks for the offer, Rayna."

"I'd love to work here," Rita enthusiastically declares. I can even start right now!"

"Thanks for the offer, but I'm pretty sure I'm moving to Connecticut," Sarah says, her hand resting on her stomach once again.

Rayna extends an open hand toward Rita in a welcoming gesture. "Then you're hired, Rita," she announces enthusiastically. "But you can start tomorrow morning. I want to give you a moment to absorb the shock of going to work and finding chains on the door." She shakes her head, her expression a mingling of pity and sadness, before turning her attention fully to me. With a curious look, Rayna asks, "And what about you, Gina?"

CHAPTER 18

The Chef's Back

RANDY

2 WEEKS LATER

THE HEAT and humidity are blistering; even my sweat is sweating as I step out from the iron gates of the sound studio onto the sunbaked concrete of New Orleans. I relish the freedom to go anywhere I want. No more reality shows for me—every moment spent filming felt like an eternity. The days and nights blurred together, my mind constantly whirring with recipes and visions of perfectly plated dishes. I'm amazed I survived the relentless schedule. The end of the show couldn't come soon enough, and the first thing I did after being released was to book my flight home. My plane leaves in less than two hours.

Scanning the street, I feel overwhelmed by the tasks that lie ahead, each one seemingly competing with the next for my attention. Relief arrives when a black SUV with tinted windows pulls up to the curb. It's my ride to the airport, arranged by the studio's reception. I hastily load my luggage into the back seat, slide in beside it, and settle in for the ride. I'm headed back to the one place I truly want to be —home, to the familiar and comforting life I left before becoming a contestant on that damn show.

The gentle rolling of the vehicle reveals how drained I truly am. It's the contradiction of sitting still while moving forward that makes my eyelids heavy. But there's a call I've needed to make, a voice I have missed hearing.

I scroll through the contacts in my cell phone until I find Gina's name, which I have labeled as "Sexy Pain In My Ass." I chuckle at the reminder of our dynamic. Running a popular restaurant kitchen teaches you to be demanding and to skip the pleasantries because things have to get done fast, and there's always too much at stake.

But at Calypso, that approach didn't fly with the staff. I remember snapping at Sarah early on and making her cry. That wasn't cool, and I knew I had to adjust my attitude. But with Gina, it was different. We sparred like equals. Her fire matched mine, especially when she would challenge me outright. Those were the moments I found myself drawn to her the most. I was enamored by her fierce spirit, the way she moved, and her kindness with customers, even the tough ones. Gina never lets anyone rattle her; she knows she's fully capable of accomplishing whatever she sets her mind to, and that's what I admire most about her.

I exhale deeply, opening my eyes as the voicemail beeps. I lean into the phone, my voice tired but clear. "Hey, beautiful, it's me, Randy. We've finished filming, and I'm on my way home. I know you're probably swamped, but if you get a chance, call me back in the next couple of hours." I pause, the longing clear in my tone. "I've missed you. Maybe we can catch up over dinner, huh? Look forward to seeing you." I end the call and lean back. The ache of missing her settles deep in my chest as the car continues speeding toward the airport.

Squeezing my phone in my hand, I can't shake a nagging feeling that I didn't say enough. I had hoped she would answer; hearing her voice would've been comforting. As I close my burning eyes, overwhelmed by a mix of disappointment and fatigue, I unexpectedly doze off. Suddenly, I'm jolted awake by the sound of my name.

"Whoa," I murmur, forcing myself to snap out of the drowsiness. Around us, the airport is bustling with the typical Sunday afternoon chaos. The driver mentions we were delayed due to a traffic accident that needed to be cleared.

When I glance at my watch, reality hits me: we're significantly behind schedule. Now I have less than forty minutes to reach my gate. The urgency heightens as I rush to check in. By the time I reach the ticket counter, only twenty minutes remain until my flight departs.

Fortunately, a twist of fate intervenes. The ticket agent recognizes me from the show, upgrades me to first class, and grants me premium check-in privileges typically reserved for celebrities. I can't help but chuckle when she calls me a celebrity; I imagine Gina standing beside me, rolling her eyes at the idea of me being regarded as one.

However, the ticket agent's next question catches me off guard. "Are you traveling with Deanna?" she asks, grinning at me conspiratorially.

"I'm flying alone," I reply.

"Oh, that's too bad. I thought you two made a cute couple." Her grin suggests she's concocted an entire romance in her mind, starring Deanna and me. It's a crazy thing, actually. I was told that's the nature of reality TV. Viewers often see what they wish to see.

Nevertheless, I express my gratitude and then rush to my gate. Even with the fast track, I barely make it before it closes. Once settled in my nice, spacious seat, a wave of relief envelops me. I'm almost home, and I can't wait to return to Gina and the Calypso.

---

3 HOURS LATER

I slept through the entire flight to LaGuardia, where I have an hour layover before the final leg to Hartford. That sleep was much needed, but I'm still exhausted. I've tried calling Steve several times, but each attempt goes straight to voicemail. Growing tired of trying to reach the people I'm calling while searching for a quick but satisfying meal, I finally call Jeremy, who answers immediately.

"So you haven't been abducted by a TV show, Jeremy jokes jubilantly. "Damn, I'm happy to hear from you."

I smile from ear to ear, glad to finally hear a familiar voice. "I couldn't call you or anyone else during production. The producers took our phones as soon as we arrived, and we had no contact with the outside world except for those, you know, associated with the show.

"Well, the outside world's been spinning off its axis," Jeremy remarks.

"Speaking of spinning, why can't I get in touch with Steve? I need him to pick me up from the airport. Where is he?"

Jeremy's prolonged silence speaks volumes, causing me to stop in my tracks. My appetite vanishes, and a chill runs down my spine as I brace myself for bad news.

"Just spit it out, Jeremy," I press him.

"All right. Brace yourself. The bank has taken possession of the Calypso and closed it down." His words hit me like a ton of bricks.

"The bad news doesn't end there," Jeremy continues. "The bank is auctioning the restaurant due to foreclosure. I tried to intervene, but it's too late. If the family wants to reacquire The Calypso, we'd have to pay a premium." He pauses. "You know what I think? Let it go. Let's move on. We kept that place running for Steve longer than we should have."

Jeremy's words clash with my instincts. I'm shaking my head because I don't agree at all. "No," I say firmly.

"Randy, you're a star after that show. Everyone's talking about you. You went there to get back on track, and you've succeeded. Go somewhere big. Blaze your trail. Stop trying to save Steve when he won't save himself."

I keep shaking my head, internally rejecting every word he's speaking. But more questions nag at me. "Where's Gina?" I ask, needing to know.

"I haven't seen her in a month or two," he replies, sounding uncertain.

"Sarah, Rita, Pete? The others? What are they doing now that the Calypso's closed?" I ask, trying to grasp the full extent of the fallout.

Jeremy's voice is tinged with impatience. "I don't know," he admits. Then, as if remembering something important, he asks, "By the way, did you win?"

The question intensifies my frown, adding a sting to my eyes. "I can't tell you that. But really, you have no idea where Steve is?"

"No, I don't," he retorts, obviously frustrated.

"How could you not know?" My voice rises slightly, a mix of disbelief and frustration coloring it.

Jeremy sighs deeply, the sound resonating in my ear. "You know, Randy, you're not doing him any favors by being codependent with him."

I jerk my head back, surprised and irritated by his accusation. "Codependent? That's a new one from you," I retort sarcastically.

Jeremy snorts facetiously. "I'm sitting in the bank, digging into my savings to bring Steve's account to zero balance. So I asked Kathy, the lovely lady I had never met until that very day, who was sitting across from me, 'What do you call it when you keep paying your cousin's gambling debts, only for him to rack up the same kind of debt again, and again, and again, and again?' And do you know what she said? 'It's called toxic codependency, and if you're involved in that kind of relationship with anyone, you need therapy.' But I don't need a therapist because I've always known what I was doing for Steve was pointless, toxic, and harmful. I've known it every time. But all my life, it's been you and Steve. You two were like brothers, which left me feeling like an outsider. I thought if I went along with this crap, maybe you'd both see me as an equal. But I'm done, Randy. I can't do it anymore."

I sigh, rubbing my throbbing temple. That was a mouthful. I've never heard Jeremy express himself like that before, and it troubles me because… "You've never been on the outside," I reply, my tone less harsh and more reassuring.

"Listen, Randy," he starts. "If we keep enabling Steve, he's just going to continue this cycle. Do you know how I found him in Atlantic City? He was begging tourists for five dollars, claiming someone stole his wallet after he lost all his money gambling." He continues, the bitterness evident. "So I asked him, 'Steve, why are you begging people for five bucks?' And he tells me, 'Because I'm on a hot streak,' and then he has the nerve to ask me for a hundred dollars.

"You know what I did next? I grabbed him by the collar, shook him, and kept repeating, 'Steve, you're out here, begging for money to gamble. You're begging for money!' Somehow, I got through to him and convinced him to come home with me. But not long after, he took money out of Calypso and was back out there in no time. So yes, I'm over it, Randy. I love him, but I'm tracking this bank sale because he's in debt up to his ears. Then I'm releasing him into the wild. Because that's where he wants to be anyway."

I take a deep breath, grounding myself before responding to Jeremy. "I understand where you're coming from," I say, my voice steady despite the turmoil inside. "But I can't step back, Jeremy. Steve's always been there for me. He's the reason I got my life back. And I know what it's like to be under Uncle Todd's roof. He was tough, not easy to love, but he did what he thought was best. It's hard to hold it against him."

I pause, thinking about the future of The Calypso, and then I make my move. "Jeremy, I want to try and save Calypso. I've got some money set aside. Can you help me work out a way to win a bid that's not going to break the bank?"

"So you did win the show?" he half-asks, half-states.

I chuckle softly, avoiding a direct answer. "I can't disclose that right now, but let's just say I'm in a position to make a serious effort. Can you help me with that?"

Jeremy sighs, a sound that tells me he disagrees with my request but isn't going to argue. "I'll do my best," he promises. Then, with a hint of concern, he asks, "So you're heading back to town?"

I look away from the gate, staring into the distance as if I can see through the crowds and miles of highways to find the one person I need to locate to be at peace right now. "After I find Steve," I reply, my voice steady with resolve.

FATE WORKS IN MYSTERIOUS WAYS. THE NEXT CALL I make is to Steve's phone, but a stranger answers. He introduces himself as Corey and explains that he bought the phone for fifty bucks from someone selling it outside a bar.

"What bar?" I urgently ask.

He names the bar, and just like that, fate steps in. It's not a surprise that Steve is in Atlantic City—a gambling addict's heaven—but the fortunate part is how simple it is for me to reroute. I decide to let my luggage fly home ahead of me, and then I opt for a $300 cab ride directly to Atlantic City. It's expensive, but it's faster than taking the train, and under the circumstances, it's worth every penny.

On my way, I call the bar and speak to a guy named Frank. I ask if he has seen someone who matches Steve's description, and luck is yet again on my side. Steve is there, drowning his sorrows in the cheapest alcohol in the house.

"I'll be there in about an hour and forty-five. Can you water down his drinks and keep him there?" I ask.

"I don't babysit," Frank replies.

I offer him $500 to change his mind. He scoffs and counters with a thousand.

"How about eight hundred?" I counteroffer.

"Deal," he agrees. "If he tries to leave, I'll have one of my guys keep an eye on him."

I feel a bit more at ease now that someone is watching my cousin. I'm not sure what state I'll find him in. Coaxing him to leave with me might be difficult, or it might be easy. Either way, he's coming home with me.

I also send a text message to Jeremy to let him know that I found our lost cousin. Even though he's had enough, I'm sure he wants to be updated.

"Where?" he quickly texts back.

I tell him the location, and after a moment, he replies, "I'm glad you found him."

I press my lips into a tight smile, knowing I was right to insist on finding Steve. And Jeremy's relieved about it too. All that talk about letting our cousin fend for himself was just pain speaking.

There's no way Jeremy could sleep easy knowing Steve might be lying in a gutter somewhere.

DURING THE TWO-HOUR CAR RIDE, I CALL GINA twice, and both times my call goes straight to voicemail. What the hell is going on? Maybe she's seeing someone else. It's possible; she is one of the most beautiful women I've ever met. I can imagine another guy rolling into town while I was away, catching her eye, and sweeping her off her feet. I always worried about that happening, yet I never made a solid move to make us exclusive. It wasn't that the thought of starting a life with her scared me—in fact, knowing her made me open to the idea of settling down, something I had never envisioned for myself before.

I'm just slow when it comes to matters of the heart, that's all. I hope she hasn't moved on with someone else. If she has, I wouldn't know what to do. All the plans I imagined for us would be wiped away, gone. This terrifying thought lingers as I stand outside a bar on the Boardwalk, peering through tall glass windows in search of that one familiar face.

It's late afternoon, and the humidity here rivals that of New Orleans. I bet it's air-conditioned inside, and I can't wait to bathe in the cold air. However, minutes ago, I sent a text to Steve's phone. I'm waiting while searching the bar, my gaze jumping from face to face, hoping for a glimpse of Steve.

"Randy?" someone calls out. I turn to see a guy who looks like a frat boy on the brink of adopting some really bad habits before turning twenty-one. He's waving at me.

I point at him. "Corey?" I ask.

He holds up Steve's cell phone, clearly not old enough to drink legally but visibly inebriated. He and his two companions probably used fake IDs to get served. Despite this, I quickly Venmo him the one hundred dollars we agreed upon. I had secured a fair price for a $2,000 iPhone by concocting a story about a low-jack security system on Steve's device. According to the tale, if the SIM card is removed without Steve's fingerprint ID, the device would implode and never work again. He bought the story and chose to recoup his fifty dollars plus an extra fifty for his time.

After that's taken care of, I step inside the bar, escaping the oppressive heat for the cooler air. The pervasive scent of alcohol hangs heavy. There was a time this would've been enticing, but now it just brings a grim reminder of darker days.

My gaze sweeps over the bar, its rectangular shape populated with patrons—none of whom are Steve. My frustration mounts, but I push it aside as I approach the bartender.

"Hey, I'm Randy. I spoke to Frank earlier about—"

"Yeah," the bartender interrupts, not needing any more details. He jerks his thumb toward the back of the room. "He couldn't sit on a stool, so we put him in a chair over there."

My gaze shifts in that direction, and relief washes over me. There's Steve, unshaven and so gaunt that he's barely recognizable. But thankfully, he's safe.

"And hey," the bartender interrupts my focus.

I quickly turn from my cousin, who's so out of it he hasn't noticed me yet, to look at the bartender.

"Frank said to keep your money," he says. "If you're willing to do this much for your family, we're happy to help for free."

I nod appreciatively. "Thank you."

"No problem," he replies before moving on to the next customer.

As I walk toward Steve, I catch murmurs from the onlookers. "Oh my God, that's Randy Thorn from the show," someone exclaims.

"What show?" another inquires.

But my focus remains fixed on my cousin. His shoulders are slumped, and he stares listlessly at his nearly full glass of piss-yellow liquid.

Finally, I sit across from Steve. Up close, he's a mess. His skin is ashen, like that of a corpse, and he struggles to lift his heavy gaze to meet mine.

My heart pounds fiercely as our eyes finally lock.

"Randy?" Steve finally asks, his voice unsure, as if he can't believe it's really me.

"Yeah, it's me," I respond, my voice tight with emotion.

Steve's shoulders begin to shake as he starts to whimper. "I didn't have my phone because I... I..." His words dissolve into sobs.

"Here it is," I say, placing his cell phone in front of him.

His sobbing pauses briefly as he stares at the phone, his face wet from tears and sweat because he's overheated from wearing too many layers in this stifling bar. He grabs the phone. "How did you get it back?"

"I made a deal with the guy you sold it to."

Visibly shaken and struggling for words, Steve shakes his head. "What have I done?"

As I rub my chin, Jeremy's words echo in my mind. I realize one thing is clear: I can't simply fix this for Steve. The thought of what needs to happen next weighs heavily on me. We can't go back to how things used to be. Starting today, we have to shift into a new reality.

I straighten up, my forearms pressing down on the table as I lean in closer to ensure that I have Steve's undivided attention. His eyes meet mine, and I hold his gaze firmly. "Where you are right now, Steve, is in the same place I was when you came and found me. It's the gutter. That's where you've landed, in the gutter." I make sure my tone is stern and unwavering.

I've learned from my own struggles that any shift in reaction can signal a breakthrough. Previously, whenever I confronted Steve about his predicament, he would dodge the issue, his eyes darting around, avoiding the truth. But this time, he continues to hold my gaze, his eyes steady and seemingly open to hearing whatever I have to say.

"Let's get you some help," I continue, believing I'm successfully getting through to him.

I watch as Steve jerks suddenly, as if waking from a daze. "Help? I can't be helped," he mutters.

"You can be helped, Steve. Anyone can be helped," I counter, keeping my tone certain despite the rush of doubt I'm experiencing. Just as fast as I thought I had him on the line and ready to bite, I'm afraid I'm starting to lose him.

He shakes his head, tears welling up in his eyes. "I'm nothing, Randy. I'm nobody. I tried, but I'm nothing."

My heart clenches at his words, anger and sorrow mingling at the self-loathing he expresses. "You can't say that, Steve," I insist, leaning closer. "You just can't say that because you are something; you are not nothing. You're sitting here in front of me, alive and breathing. You have ten fingers, ten toes, a brain, a heart, blood pumping through your veins. That alone proves you're a living being. So don't ever say you're nothing because that's not true. You're saying that because that's how you feel, and feelings aren't always reality. You've tried gambling to escape those memories that you carry in your mind and in your body. You've tried booze. But none of that will ever stop the lies you keep telling yourself." My words have tumbled out rapidly, a torrent of hope and desperation, and now

I have to catch my breath, hoping he really hears me this time. "Get help, Steve," I continue. "It's the only way you'll see your true worth. I did it. That's what I had to do. Look at me now."

I jump, startled, as a gentle hand suddenly grasps my shoulder, the touch familiar. "Well said," a familiar voice murmurs.

Steve lifts his heavy-lidded gaze, tracking Jeremy as he settles in to the empty chair beside him.

"I was in New York City when you called," Jeremy explains, mentioning his flight from Teterboro.

I acknowledge how thankful I am that he came with a nod.

There's a brief silence as we all absorb the significance of our gathering.

"I'm ready," Steve whispers, his fatigue evident in his voice. "It's time."

CHAPTER 19

Cat's Out of the Bag

RANDY

THIS MORNING, I struggle to even stand on my feet. Throughout the final hours of filming, the thought of going home, seeing Gina, and finally getting some rest propelled me forward. But now, the reality is far from what I imagined. Yesterday, Jeremy and I checked Steve into the same rehab center that helped me recover. The future is uncertain—whether the treatment will work for him this time is unclear. It's all up to Steve now; his journey is his own.

Steve's recent decision brings a glimmer of hope. Thank goodness for Jeremy and his lawyer. Because of their thorough examination of the loan agreement, we discovered that Steve could transfer his loan to another individual if the overdue balance was settled within forty-five days of default. When Jeremy paid off Steve's debt, he inadvertently met the deadline. Long story short, yesterday, Steve agreed to transfer the mortgage to me, and I've deposited the balance of the loan into an escrow account. Soon, ownership of Calypso will be mine.

It's odd standing outside Calypso, seeing chains and a hefty black padlock securing the doors. Even though it's a disheartening moment, I'm eager to step inside and breathe in the familiar scent of the place once again. The anticipation of wandering through the kitchen, knowing it belongs to me, is exciting.

I have ideas to turn our town into a culinary hotspot, beginning with my own restaurant. My ambitions go beyond just my own establishment. I want to work with other restaurants who are interested in transforming their menus and services. By improving the dining experience throughout our town, visitors drawn by my restaurant will also discover the variety of delicious foods our community has to offer. My hope is that our collective effort will make our town a prime destination for food lovers.

My ambitious goals prompted me to reach out to Deanna to ask if she's willing to support me in taking on this monumental task. We talked about my next steps after the show ended. She suggested I go back to New York and start my own restaurant. I assured her that this place, this town, is where I belong.

"All right, Randy," she said, pacifying me. "You're tired. Go home, rest, and we'll revisit this conversation in a month or two."

Neither of us could've guessed that I would've bought the Calypso. When I pitched to her my plan to make this town a culinary pit stop, she didn't shut me down.

"Will Jeremy be involved?" she quipped.

I couldn't help but smirk at the mental image of her playfully batting her eyelashes at Jeremy.

Keeping the conversation honest, I responded, "Only if we need his business acumen."

"But I need *him*." She snorted with laughter. "Well, not really *need*, but I definitely *want* him. So what's the deal with him these days? Has he found a girlfriend yet?"

"Not yet," I replied. Our longstanding friendship and her role as my formidable manager have always been built on honesty, which is why I have to tell her the whole truth. "You know, I told him you're interested, but he's just not looking for a relationship at the moment, although he is flattered."

Deanna let out a cynical laugh. "Ah, 'flattered.' That's the polite way of saying 'thanks, but no thanks.' But yeah, count me in."

Her response was a huge weight off my shoulders. Deanna is a seasoned expert in launching, sustaining, and popularizing restaurants and chefs. If she ever claimed credit for making Chef Randy Thorn, it wouldn't be a fib. She'd be stating the unvarnished truth. As my manager, she took a leap of faith when nobody else would. Even during my lowest moments, she stood by me unwaveringly. I owe much of my success in the competition to her. Without her guidance, I doubt I would have made it as far as I did.

Discovering she was a fellow contestant on the show came as a shock. When another chef dropped out, production asked her to step in. While a heads-up would have been nice, having her there was an advantage. She coached me through the challenges, kept my spirits high, and reminded me of what was at stake, just as any effective manager would. Her presence was a reassuring force throughout the competition.

A blue sedan, followed closely by a white pickup

truck, glides into the parking lot. I wave at Deanna, who is behind the wheel of the sedan. Despite the early hour, she made the journey from Boston and spent the morning at the local bank, working tirelessly to ensure the doors would be unchained today. While part of me longed to remain snug in bed for the next twenty-four hours, I knew that if anyone could accomplish getting us the keys and inside before the bureaucracy was finalized, it was Deanna. Sure enough, she managed to get it done.

"Randy, Dandy," she calls out as she emerges from the driver's seat, exuding brightness and cheerfulness. Deanna seems well-rested, having had a full night's sleep ahead of me.

"Grr," I playfully groan, earning a laugh from her.

However, the closer she gets, the more concerned she looks. "You look terrible," she says.

"Physically, I feel terrible," I admit. "But inside, I'm throwing a party, overjoyed that he's here with those." I gesture toward the keys in the hand of the individual who will soon unlock the door to my new restaurant and allow us to step inside.

WITH A NEWFOUND SPRING IN MY STEP, I LEAD Deanna through our walk-through of the establishment. The place needs a thorough cleaning—that's for sure. I catch sight of a bunch of soiled aprons, towels, and tablecloths hanging on hooks, awaiting the night cleaning service that never came.

Yet the spirit of this place still lives on. I can almost feel the presence of the former employees, who are now my friends, when we reach the locker room. The locker Gina often uses catches my eye, serving as a reminder that we need to talk soon. I simply want to know why she's dodging my calls.

Deanna estimates the square footage of the space we're standing in and suggests that we eliminate the locker room to expand the dining area, which often becomes overcrowded. Despite the many cherished memories I've made in this room, including those nights when Gina and I made love on the bench or against the wall, I find myself agreeing with her suggestion.

"Hello?" a curious voice calls out from the front, interrupting our conversation.

Deanna and I exchange raised eyebrows, both wondering who could be visiting at this hour. It certainly isn't Gina or any of the former staff.

"Maybe it's a customer mistaking us for being

open since the doors are unlocked," Deanna says. "I'll go check it out."

"No, I'll handle it," I insist, quickly moving to address our unexpected visitor.

As I approach, I come to an abrupt halt upon recognizing the person standing before me. "Naomi?" I ask, surprised to see Gina's best friend here.

Initially, I entertain the thought that Naomi might have mistaken the restaurant for being open. But then, a chilling realization sets in. Maybe it's something else. Could something be seriously wrong with Gina, and that's why she hadn't answered my calls? Has Naomi spotted my car in the parking lot and come inside to deliver the bad news that Gina's in the hospital, or worse? The mere thought sends a shiver down my spine.

"What's going on?" I ask, my tone laced with caution and worry.

To my relief, Naomi responds with a bright smile that perfectly matches her usually sunny disposition. "I was just in the neighborhood and noticed the doors were open, so I decided to see what's going on," she explains. "I'm actually moving to Boston." Her gaze drifts nostalgically around the familiar surroundings. "I've spent so much time in here over the years."

I'm taken aback by the nostalgia in her voice as she reminisces about the past. She recounts the countless times she visited Gina while she was on a break and how I seemingly kept track of every second of Gina's downtime. She chuckles as she mentions it, but I find myself questioning—did I really monitor her every moment?

"But you're back!" she exclaims as if just realizing the surprise of encountering me here.

"I am," I manage to reply softly. While I could engage in small talk about my plans to reopen the restaurant after renovations, I can't shake the feeling that Naomi walking in here is akin to Gina herself walking in, given their inseparable bond. If anyone truly knows why Gina has been avoiding my calls or if she's involved with someone else, it's the woman standing before me.

Part of me desperately wants to ask about Gina, but at the same time, I'm terrified of what the answer might be. Will it destroy me from the inside out?

"Hello?" Deanna's voice chimes in as she enters the front of the restaurant.

Naomi's eyes widen in horror. "Oh," she says, looking at Deanna as if she's just seen a ghost. "So it *is* true."

"What's true?" Deanna and I ask at the same time.

"You two are… You know?" Naomi stammers, her finger wagging between us.

"You know what?" Deanna asks as she walks over to stand beside me. Then she turns to face me. "Randy, the strangest thing happened on my flight home. A few people asked if you and I were together. I didn't think anything of it at first; I just assumed they were fans drawing their own conclusions. But…"

"Me too," I interject, recollecting my own encounter with the ticket agent.

"What the hell is going on?" Deanna exclaims, folding her arms and focusing her attention on Naomi as if she's the only one capable of answering her question.

"Yeah, why would you think I'm hooking up with Deanna?" I ask, puzzled by the implication.

"Okay, I'm not that horrible," Deanna retorts, picking up on my tone.

"Sorry, D. You're a beautiful lady, but us being together is pretty unlikely. We're like family."

She nods in agreement. "Extremely unlikely."

Now both of us fix our curious gazes on Naomi, awaiting an explanation.

"Well," she begins, then proceeds to tell us about the show and how, during our interviews, we mentioned our past relationship. She says that although we never explicitly stated that we were romantically involved, it seemed clear that we were playing coy about it.

"We never said that or played coy," Deanna snaps, her frustration evident.

"Never," I confirm, equally irked by the misunderstanding.

"Those assholes must've stitched scenes together to create the narrative they wanted people to see," Deanna hisses.

"But you slapped him on the butt and—" Naomi begins, trying to explain.

"Yes," Deanna interrupts irritably. "I told him to get his ass in gear because he was lagging behind and needed to win the challenge. I was a contestant, but I'm not the star chef; he is," she exclaims, clearly upset. "Sorry," she adds, shaking her head. "I'm not mad at you. I'm mad at those snakes for creating this narrative without running it by me first for approval. I wouldn't have given it because he's my star client. They're messing with my reputation." Deanna unleashes a string of expletives before pressing two fingers to her temples and taking deep, calming breaths.

I raise my eyebrows at Naomi, who appears shocked by Deanna's reaction.

"I didn't… we didn't… Oh my God," Naomi whispers, clearly taken aback by the situation.

"So is that what's going on? That's why Gina's not answering my calls?" I ask her. "She thinks I'm in a relationship with Deanna?"

With a resolved sigh, Naomi nods. "But it's more than that."

For a moment, I feel a glimmer of relief, but it's quickly overshadowed by worry. If that damn show has cost me the chance with the only woman I've ever truly loved, I'll sue their asses—if I can. "What more? Is she with someone else?" I ask, bracing myself for the worst.

"No," Naomi replies convincingly. "It's just that I can't tell you, although I think you should know."

"Not with another man…" Deanna murmurs, as if trying to solve a puzzle. "Can't tell him, but thinks he should know…" Her eyes widen in realization, and she clamps a hand over her mouth.

I shake my head, still confused by the cryptic conversation unfolding before me.

And then Deanna blurts it out. "She's pregnant, Randy!"

I'm stunned into silence. My hand instinctively goes to my chest as I feel a surge of sensations swelling inside—it's akin to butterflies fluttering wildly within me.

Naomi raises her hands in a gesture of innocence. "I didn't say it—it was Deanna," she clarifies, gesturing toward Deanna. "Remember, if Gina asks, it wasn't me."

"I'm heading to her place now," I announce, poised to rush out the door.

"She moved out," Naomi blurts just as I'm about to exit. "And she's not home right now."

"Where is she, then?" I ask, my body tensing, ready to sprint off like the wind as soon as I know where to find the woman I love.

CHAPTER 20

He Loves Me

GINA

On mornings like this, I find myself questioning the decision I made about Rayna's job offer. I proposed a similar arrangement to her as the one I had with Calypso: baking in her kitchen overnight following the podcast day and selling pastries during their morning rush. Unfortunately, even though this setup could potentially bring more customers to her business, she didn't have enough staff to handle the increase. However, Rayna was open to the idea of gradually expanding her operations and wanted me to be a part of that growth.

She gave me a week to consider her offer, which I graciously declined after my graduation ceremony from culinary school last weekend. While my graduation might not have been as prestigious as Naomi's law school, it held equal significance for me. Receiving my certificate and hearing my instructors call me one of their most gifted students brought a moment of clarity. I realized that I wanted to focus more on expanding the business that stemmed from the podcast.

My parents supported this decision wholeheartedly; my father even secured a new venue where I could sell my pastries that Monday. That place is Fannie's Flowers, where Ms. Fannie is thrilled to host me. Since I've started setting up shop in her store twice a week, her florist business has flourished.

Now each episode night, I manage to catch four to five hours of sleep before waking up to bake into the early morning. After another quick two or three hours of rest, I load the baked goods into a van uniquely decorated to promote the podcast. It has images of the four smiling hosts on one side. Gina, the baker—me—delicately decorating a macaron, adorns the other side. This van, a thoughtful purchase by my dad, not only transports my pastries to Fannie's Flowers but also shuttles podcast hosts to promotional events across town and throughout the state.

Yes, the ladies have become quite popular, and a

significant part of their appeal seems to be linked to my participation in their conversations. My discomfort is evidently clear, and it turns out that older viewers enjoy seeing how uneasy the ladies make me. Apparently, those my age appreciate watching me stand up to them while being both respectful and assertive. However, I still try to stick to the baking, keep my head down, and stay out of the table talk as much as possible.

Oddly, at this very moment, I find myself distracted by their podcast topic, which is why I feel as though I want to be anywhere else but here. As I methodically measure flour and crack eggs, the conversation turns unexpectedly personal—Bree, Carrie's unmarried daughter, is pregnant. I've always known that one day, a podcast topic might inch narrowly close to my own predicament, and today it is happening.

Here's the situation as it unfolded a moment ago:

Joyce, never one for subtlety, blurted out, "Well, how far along is she?"

Carrie's response came through clenched teeth and narrowed eyes. "I don't know because she kept it a secret from us."

Under my breath, I muttered, "Maybe because she didn't want to be the subject of gossip."

Unfazed by the tension, Linda, devoid of any tact, pressed further. "She hid it? Who's the father?"

Now we're engulfed in the prolonged silence that follows. Carrie seems to have shrunk into her chair. Despite being the one who brought up the topic, it's clear she wishes it would disappear just as quickly, away from the prying eyes and ears of the other women.

"I don't know," Carrie finally responds, her voice low and her demeanor reluctant. "Apparently, she doesn't tell me anything anymore." Her arms are crossed tightly against her chest, her body language almost protesting her own words.

I can predict her next move, and sure enough, Carrie turns to me. "What do you think, Gina?"

As I stir vanilla extract into my brown butter cream, I feel my cheeks burn. I understand why Carrie has directed this question at me. I've noticed a recurring activity: whenever the conversation veers into negative territory about one of their children, the mothers tend to draw me into the discussion, expecting me to offer a defense on their offspring's behalf. I'm not even sure they're aware they do this, but here I am, put on the spot as their curious eyes remain fixed on me.

Meeting their gazes, my brain attempts to churn out the right response. Should I reveal that I'm in the same boat as Carrie? I knew her in high school, but she and I ran in totally different circles, being that she was two grades higher than me. My scandalous secret would certainly take the heat off Carrie. All this time, while baking, selling, and making public appearances, I've been pregnant too. But am I ready to disclose the identity of the father —Randy Thorn, the man they've predicted will ride off into the sunset with the flawless Deanna Blume? *No way.*

Realizing I can't prolong my silence any longer, I finally open my mouth to speak. After another brief pause, I know what must be said. "I don't know, Carrie," I start with a flippant shrug. "Maybe Bree felt it was safer keeping the information to herself."

Carrie's expression crumbles into a deep frown, fierce enough to intimidate the boogeyman. "Of course I'm safe!" she snaps, her frustration evident. "Who's safer to tell than her own mother?"

I nearly respond with a sharp comment about the relentless dirt-dishing that goes on at their table and suggest that maybe her daughter is withholding news because of it. But I hold back, opting for a more tactful approach. "Listen, Carrie, there are many reasons why someone might keep a pregnancy private initially. For example, some prefer to wait until they're past the first trimester before sharing the news, just to ensure everything is progressing okay."

The ladies nod in agreement, each acknowledging the validity of the point. I'm relieved and certain my diplomatic response got them off my back for the time being.

"But didn't she eventually tell you?" Joyce asks Carrie. "She must have said something for you to find out."

Carrie's face turns a deep shade of red, and I instantly regret the turn the conversation has taken. It's clear she discovered her daughter's pregnancy in a less than ideal way.

"I called her, and somehow, I heard her speaking to someone. She didn't know she had answered my call," Carrie confesses, clearly puzzled by the incident.

"Ah, a butt dial or something," Norie suggests, nodding confidently as if she's familiar with the concept.

"No," I mutter under my breath, knowing they can't hear me.

"Yes, that's it," my mom agrees, mistakenly confirming the incorrect term for what likely happened. I suspect that Bree thought she had silenced her mom's call but accidentally answered it instead.

Joyce slaps the table. "Well, there you go. She's talking to her friend about it before saying anything to you," she deduces a bit too bluntly.

Carrie falls silent once more, retreating inwardly.

I sigh, shaking my head. Joyce's observation, though accurate, has clearly stung Carrie. Seeing her hurt, I contemplate whether it's time to share my own secret.

Before I can say anything, my mom speaks up. "Maybe she just didn't want her special news shared with the entire world."

"What do you mean, Faye?" Carrie demands.

Despite her cohost's defensive tone, my mom doesn't back down. "We must take responsibility for gossiping about the parts of our kids' lives that they might prefer to keep private. That's all I'm saying. We enjoy the stories, sure, but there could be a price," she explains calmly yet firmly.

"We're not gossiping," Joyce retorts sharply, likely defensive because she's the most frequent gossip of the group.

"Oh, you're gossiping," I blurt out, unable to hold my tongue any longer.

The shocked expressions they direct at me make me feel as if I've been caught stealing the last truffle-infused grilled cheese sandwich my mom prepares before every Thursday podcast. They really love those sandwiches.

"Gina!" a man's voice booms, slicing through the tension.

All eyes, previously fixed on me, turn in unison. Standing before us is Chef Randy Thorn, his presence as striking as ever. The surprise of seeing him causes me to release the teaspoon of baking soda I had been holding between my fingers.

"Randy?" I barely whisper, finding my voice again.

He approaches me cautiously, his hands raised, palms out in a gesture of peace. "Gina, I know you're pregnant," he declares, unintentionally disclosing my secret to the very people I had hoped to keep it from.

I catch a brief glimpse of the ladies as they

erupt in gasps, but I can't focus on them for long; I'm too stunned by Randy's presence.

"Gina, you're not pregnant, are you?" my dad asks, his expression clouded with uncertainty.

The heartbreak in his eyes is upsetting, and even more so when I see his shoulders sag as he reads the truth in mine. I know I owe my parents a thorough explanation, but that will have to wait. Right now, my attention is torn between the concern on my dad's face and Randy, who is steadily approaching us.

It's Randy who captures my full attention, as he's all I can see. "Babe..." he starts. My gaze locks onto every detail of his face. The dark circles under his eyes contrast starkly with his gaunt complexion. He looks utterly exhausted. "I've been missing you terribly," he confesses.

"How did you find out I was pregnant?" I decide to ask outright, now that the secret is already out.

"I knew she was hiding something," Joyce declares victoriously, her voice rising as she punctuates her triumph with a loud hand clap.

"Gina? Are you truly pregnant?" My mom's upset voice cuts through the tension-filled air that has settled around us.

"Please, Mrs. Emerson, could I finish?" Randy respectfully asks. "I've been practicing what I want to say to your daughter on the drive over, and I don't want to forget it."

Silenced by the moment, I watch my mom. Though anguished, she gives Randy the nod to continue. The backyard falls quiet with anticipation.

Randy clears his throat. "It seems the world believes there's something going on between Deanna Blume and me. But aside from our longstanding friendship and her role as my business manager, there's nothing else."

"Then why were you cozying up to her?" Joyce's voice rings out, capturing everyone's attention.

Randy and I quickly turn to face her.

"That's a great question, Joyce," Linda chimes in, nodding in agreement to emphasize her point.

"There was no cozying up, I assure you," Randy responds firmly.

"But you and Deanna Blume were romantically linked, at least at one point, weren't you?" Norie interjects, her arms crossed defiantly as if she's skeptical of his denial.

The scene feels almost surreal. It's as if the

ladies have spontaneously decided to interview him, each one eager to probe deeper.

Randy's face tightens into a deep frown, weariness etched into his features. "Deanna and I were never romantically linked."

"That's not what you said on the show," Norie retorts.

He shakes his head, and I can see in his eyes that he's desperately looking for a way out of this unexpected interrogation.

But just as I'm about to intervene, he says, "They asked me questions during interviews, but my guess is they twisted my words to make the show more interesting. I would have thought the cooking alone was interesting enough since I really gave it my all."

"But she slapped you on the rear end!" Carrie interjects, as if that single action undermines Randy's explanation.

"Yes. She was encouraging me to get moving. That challenge was particularly tough, and I was falling behind," Randy explains.

Carrie tilts her head skeptically. "But she jumped into your arms, and you spun her around," she presses on, her tone insistent, demanding further clarification.

"Oh," Randy responds, nodding as if the memory has just clicked into place. "Yes, that was right after I won the second competition. As my manager, she was really pumped, whispering in my ear, 'We're back, we're back, we're so back.'" Suddenly he stiffens, appearing conflicted, then scratching the back of his head, he says, "I don't think I can say more about what happened on the show. I signed an NDA, and I'm pretty sure I said too much already."

Gradually, all five hosts nod, seeming to accept his explanation. Relief washes over me. Randy has weathered their relentless questioning and emerged unscathed.

"So, you didn't win?" my mom asks abruptly.

Her inquiry clearly catches Randy off guard. He hesitates, visibly conflicted. "Again, I can't say, Mrs. Emerson. Even though I really want to answer you… I just can't." Fatigue is evident in his voice.

Before anyone else can jump in with more questions, I interject firmly. "I believe him." I say it again, more emphatically, to silence any doubts. "I believe him." My voice is urgent and breathless.

Randy and I lock gazes as he steps closer, now just within reach. I pull him toward me, closing the distance. At this moment, the rest of the world seems to fade away, leaving just the two of us.

"That was rough," he whispers, his voice light with a chuckle.

I let out a breathy laugh in response. "Yeah. Sorry about that."

"No," he shakes his head gently, frowning earnestly. "Don't be. I want you to know that the only woman I'm in love with is you."

Tears well up in my eyes as I whisper back, "I love you too."

Randy's fingers gently stroke the side of my neck, and I lean into his tender touch, feeling a rush of shivers down my spine.

"Hi," he whispers, his voice thick with emotion.

Tears streaming down my cheeks, I muster a joyful, "Hi."

Our lips seem to pull toward each other like magnets, but we restrain ourselves, knowing this isn't the place or time for more. Instead, we simply beam at each other as he tenderly wipes the tears from my face.

"You need help with this?" he asks, nodding toward my workstation.

"Okay," I manage to whisper, my throat tight with emotion.

Just then, my mom's voice cuts through the air. "Alrighty then," she begins, perhaps attempting to lighten the mood. "Keeping with our standards, I guess it's my turn to dish about my daughter." It's hard to tell if she's trying to be funny. Her tone shifts as she continues. "So why do you think it has taken two months for my daughter, who I have a very good relationship with, to tell me she's pregnant?" Her question hangs in the air, clearly not meant as a joke. She's genuinely upset.

Taking a deep, steadying breath, I realize it's time to address everyone—my parents, the ladies, and even the listeners. "I'm sorry, everybody. Should've, would've, could've, but I'm only human. It was hard to accept that the man I am deeply attracted to and have fallen in love with was portrayed as falling for another woman…"

Joyce cuts me off with a question. "How long have you two known each other?"

Surprised, I jerk my head back. Are they even listening to my apology? Randy and I exchange perplexed frowns, thrown off by the sudden shift.

"A year," I respond, still a bit flustered.

"Thirteen months and twenty-three days," Randy specifies more accurately.

"Are you going to marry her?" Carrie interjects abruptly.

My eyes widen in shock, nearly popping from their sockets as I gasp, horrified by the bluntness of her question.

Before I can shut down this line of questioning, Randy answers with a calm and steady, "Yes. One day, yes. That's if she'll have me." Suddenly, he stiffens like a strong thought just came to mind. "I'm sorry," he begins, and then he turns his attention to my mom and then dad. "Mrs. and Mr. Emerson, with all due respect, I can't wait any longer. I need to kiss your daughter. And I've been missing her badly, so it's going to be really juicy. Can you handle it?"

First, my parents exchange a look, silently checking in with each other.

My mom's grin then stretches from ear to ear as she enthusiastically replies, "We can handle it."

My dad, with a slightly more restrained smile, gives a thumbs-up.

And so, I'm soon feeling as if I'm floating on air as I become reacquainted with the taste of Randy's mouth, the pressure of his tongue indulging in mine, his lips slipping passionately between my lips, and soon his excitement can be felt in all the right places.

CHAPTER 21

If Even By Accident

The drive to Randy's house is torturous. We make out at every stoplight, although there aren't many because he doesn't live that far from my parents' house. We quickly catch up on each other's lives. Yes, Randy is running on fumes and has hardly slept since being released from the show. He shares how the lack of sleep and the physical demands have taken a toll on him, and he's surprised he managed to make it through. Then in an unexpected twist, he reveals that he has purchased the Calypso Café.

My mouth falls open in shock, and all I can manage is a bewildered, "What?"

Randy explains that Jeremy used his savvy to navigate the bureaucracy and discovered that Steve, who is currently in rehab, still had the chance to transfer his loan to another borrower. Taking advantage of this opportunity, Steve transferred the mortgage to Randy, who promptly paid off the remaining loan amount.

"So you did win!" I shriek, realization dawning on me.

With a shrewd wink and a grin that lights up his weary face, I know the answer before he even speaks. Raising his eyebrows, he asks, "Can we keep this between us?"

"Yay, you won!" I erupt, clapping in celebration, unable to contain my excitement.

To that, Randy reclaims one of my hands, raises the back of it to his lips, and declares, "I missed you like crazy." He then plants a sweet kiss on my knuckles before announcing that he is the new *Head Chef Total Domination* champ.

Unable to stop smiling, I say, "I knew you would be crowned the champion."

"Thanks, babe."

Beaming, I ask, "I'm really your babe?"

"Yes. And I'm yours."

We lock eyes, caught in a moment of deep connection, until Randy has to focus back on the road. It's still surreal to me that I'm here with

Randy Thorn like this. But it's undeniable—we're officially a couple.

"How do you feel, you know, being pregnant?" he asks, breaking into my thoughts.

Caught up in the joy of being with him and the electric connection between us, I'd almost forgotten about our impending parenthood. "Fine," I reply in a high-pitched, optimistic voice.

"It must've been hard for you to believe I was with someone else," he continues.

"Very," I admit, letting go of the past discomfort that plagued me before Randy's bold declaration of commitment and love.

He asks how often I see the doctor, and I fill him in about my visits with Dr. Haskell, my yoga routine, and the careful diet I've been following lately. He's pleased to hear I'm taking care of myself and expresses his eagerness to start taking care of me together. That statement makes me want to jump his bones even more.

Thank goodness he turns into the long driveway. The house is striking with its gorgeous brick and barn-red craftsman style, but it also looks like the perfect home to raise a family. Out of patience and eager to get things heated, we head directly into the house. Once inside, I feel like I'm walking on air as Randy takes my hand and ceremoniously leads me to the master bedroom.

This space is so him. The neutral grays and greens create a calm and sophisticated atmosphere. His bed is king-sized, and the frame and backboard are made of light sheet wood. His taste is minimalistic.

So quickly, we strip out of our clothes until we're standing naked on a plush, off-white, faux fur area rug, facing each other. He's so hot, and I'm so eager to touch him that I spread my hands against his sculpted chest.

"Hey, you," Randy whispers throatily.

The anticipation of what's to come is making me dizzy. My "Hey" comes out throaty too.

Randy moves a wayward lock of hair from my forehead. "There," he says. "Now I can see you better."

My body tingles with longing as our front sides finally make skin-on-skin contact. But Randy keeps gazing into my eyes, restraining himself for some reason. He has never made me wait like this before he makes the fiery first move. I want him to take me already. To encourage him, I lift my heels so that I'm standing on my tiptoes. I stop just before our lips touch and wait for him to take the bait.

And he does.

Within a split second, our passions carry forward like a locomotive leaving the station, picking up speed. I grab him by the back of the head and bring his mouth closer to mine. Breathing heavily, Randy pulls back as if unaware he has stopped. Eyes revealing intense lust, he only studies me for a second before pulling my hair downward. His hooded gaze feasts on the skin of my exposed neck. I moan with need before his mouth and tongue devour my throat, tasting me thoroughly. And then we erupt in flames of passion as we tumble onto the bed, kissing, petting, pushing. Finally, I open up, and he enters me. Raising my hips to meet his, we make love like our lives depend on it.

MANY HOURS LATER

It's early the next morning. Throughout the night, Randy's tongue managed to taste and stimulate every inch of my body, and mine did the same for him. Even though he was worn out from the competition, Randy impressively made love to me so many times that my body still feels limp, worn out from the exercise of hot, passionate sex.

As I fully open my eyes, I'm greeted by a window framed with drawn curtains. The tall, healthy trees surrounding the property filter the morning sun rising in the east, casting a comfortable light that fills the room. This soothing ambiance makes me snuggle deeper into Randy, who is gently snoring beside me. Yielding to the peaceful moment, I allow myself to drift back into sleep.

"UMM…" RANDY'S MOAN TRAVELS DEEP IN MY EAR canal, and then I feel his lips on the back of my shoulder. Then his manhood thrusts against me and inside me. We're off for another round of lovemaking.

MANY MORE HOURS LATER

Randy and I are laughing uncontrollably, the sound echoing around us. I revel in the feeling of his body shaking with laughter against mine. It strikes me that this is the first time I've truly heard him laugh. Until now, our interactions have always been so serious. I'm really enjoying discovering this lighter, more joyful side of Randy. It feels like we've always had the potential to be just as we are now—relaxed and genuine with each other.

"You were brutal," he reminisces, referring to a dinner party we attended over a year ago.

It was Naomi's and Derek's post-engagement announcement dinner, a playful event Naomi coined simply to capture the joy of planning gatherings with friends alongside the man she intended to marry one day.

I told her she was off her rocker, naturally. But that's Naomi for you. She swings from one extreme to the other—from being very pragmatic and practical to embracing the carefree and adventurous. That's just her way, and I love it.

I had no idea Naomi would invite Randy. She had run the guest list by me multiple times before that night, and Randy's name was never mentioned. So you can imagine my shock when I arrived and saw him sitting at the table with the nine of us—close friends of Derek's and shared friends of Naomi and me.

In my surprise, I pulled Naomi aside and grilled her about his unexpected presence. We were alone in the kitchen when I demanded an explanation.

"Because he's a cool addition to any dinner party, Gina," she casually said.

"How do you even know that?" I countered, feeling my frustration rise. "You barely know him."

"Gina," Naomi said, taking me by the shoulders to steady me. "Chill out."

"I am chilled out," I snapped back, clearly not as composed as I claimed.

That's when I caught the mischievous glimmer in her eyes and the naughty smirk curving her lips.

"You're not playing matchmaker here, are you?" I accused, half-joking yet half-serious.

"No!" She sang out her denial a bit too high-pitched to be convincing. "Gina, he's sitting so far away from you. You don't even have to look at him if you don't want to."

The truth was, Naomi was indeed playing matchmaker, but not for me. It was for Sadie McPherson, a legal assistant at Derek's law firm. Sadie thought Randy was attractive and wanted to make her interest known, just like every other single woman in town seemed to. Did that bother me?

Looking back now, I admit that it probably did just a teensy-weensy bit.

The seating arrangement was just as Naomi had promised. Everyone was positioned around the family farm-style table, with Sadie sitting directly across from Randy and me at the far end, opposite our friend Tanya. I had managed not to glance at Randy too much, but it was hard not to steal looks to see if Sadie was making any headway with him. At that time, Randy had been at Calypso for only a month. Our interactions often involved a lot of snappy exchanges, and while there was undeniable sexual tension simmering beneath the surface, we were far from acting on it.

Soon, the first course was served, and the table talk began. The opening question was a challenging one: "What on your bucket list have you already fulfilled?"

I was relieved they hadn't started with me, though I knew my turn would inevitably arrive. Internally, I scrambled to think of an answer. If Randy hadn't been there, I doubt I would have cared much about sharing the truth. Others at the table boasted about experiences like skydiving and the thrill of free-falling through the sky, or horseback riding, which they had avoided due to a fear of horses. Dinner guests erupted in laughter when someone revealed they recently ticked a hot dog eating contest off the list. Amidst the laughter, I grappled with whether to be honest.

"Okay, Gina, you're next," Naomi announced, clapping her hands to signal it was my turn to share.

I wished I could have said "pass." From the first day, Randy's presence made me feel as though I was constantly playing catch-up, living a life less full than his. As the question came to me, my mind raced, desperately searching for an answer. Unable to find a truthful response, I finally said, "Riding in a hot air balloon."

"Humph." Randy's voice was loud enough for the entire table to turn their heads in curiosity.

That single sound was enough to set me off. "What do you mean by, 'humph'?" I snapped, frustration evident in my tone.

"Nothing," he replied casually.

My eyes burned as I glared at him, unconvinced. "Oh, it's definitely something."

He shifted uncomfortably in his chair. "I just didn't expect you to say that, that's all."

"What did you expect me to say?" I pressed.

"Why does what I think matter so much to you?" he shot back, the question hanging in the air.

I remember frowning deeply at that moment as I took stock of myself. I was leaning across a friend of Derek's who was seated next to me—someone Derek had later mentioned he'd intended to set me up with, though I hadn't even noticed him. To this day, I can't recall what he looked like.

Feeling embarrassed by my irrational fervor and realizing that Randy had posed a valid question, I straightened up. I noticed the surprised looks from everyone at the table and retreated into myself. I was done talking. Naomi, who never liked to put me on the spot in public, would later ask, "When did you take a hot air balloon ride?" I had to admit, "Never," and explain that I couldn't think of anything else to say in the moment.

The guy next to me mentioned he had hiked at a place called Whitney Portal, which impressed many at the table. As the conversation moved on, I couldn't stop kicking myself for not just sharing my truth. Lying so frivolously wasn't like me at all.

"My adventure in Marrakech," Randy announced when it was his turn.

I burst out with cynical laughter and blurted, "Okay, right?"

The other guests and hosts looked at me as if I had lost my mind. Couldn't they see what was happening here, I wondered.

Leaning forward so he could better see me, Randy asked, "Is that funny to you?"

"You're just so pompous," I blurted out, unable to hold back.

Randy huffed, clearly agitated. I had effectively lured him into matching my energy. "You know what? I get what your problem with me is. Why don't you show up to work on time, and maybe I won't be so pompous?"

We engaged in what felt like the stare-off of the century. If I'm being honest, I felt more inclined to gouge his eyes out than to kiss him.

Then, suddenly, he jumped, startled by the vibration of his cell phone. Pulling it from his pocket, he frowned at the screen. Whatever he saw seemed to disturb him. He quickly apologized to Naomi and Derek and excused himself, saying he had to take the call.

Randy lifted his eyebrows at me, a clear sign that our skirmish was over. Then Naomi raised her eyebrows inquisitively at me as if to ask, "What in the world is wrong with you?"

I just shrugged, silently communicating my

regret and confusion over my own behavior.

Shortly thereafter, Randy returned to the table, but not for long. With a serious expression, he announced that he had a family emergency and excused himself from the dinner. It took every ounce of my self-control not to scoff at his excuse. For some reason, I found it hard to believe him. My mind conjured up scenarios of him rushing off to meet some hot date instead. I convinced myself that he found our small-town company and our mundane dinner party questions too dull.

"Where did you go anyway?" I ask, nestled safely in Randy's arms as he holds me close in bed.

"That was the day Jeremy's divorce was finalized. He was having a tough time, so I drove out to Boston to be with him."

A memory flickers in my mind. "That's right. You didn't come in the next day."

"No," Randy murmurs softly, planting a delicate, warm kiss on the back of my neck. "But I have something for you."

I feel a chill as he pulls away; the absence of his warmth is immediate. My gaze follows him to a chic floating dresser. He rummages through the top right drawer and pulls out a folded piece of lined paper.

I sit up, intrigued. "What's that?"

"It's my bucket list. The real one." Randy stands at the foot of the bed, holding the paper. "But before we unfold this, I want to clarify something." He tilts his head, a curious look in his eyes. "Really? A hot air balloon ride?"

I throw my head back, laughing heartily. "No," I enthusiastically admit. "I totally made that up. I don't have a bucket list," I confess. "I just live in the moment."

Randy's knees press into the mattress as he moves closer, his eyes smoldering with intensity. He leans in, and we share a deep, sweet, loving kiss.

"I knew that," he whispers as our lips part. He then makes himself comfortable next to me against the headboard. "I didn't have a bucket list either. I never even thought about one until that night."

I sit up straighter in surprise. "You mean you've never been to Marrakech?"

"Yes, I have. But it was to taste food and explore the spices—purely work, not play. But…" He hands me the folded piece of paper. "Read it."

I carefully unfold the paper, my heart beating with anticipation. Randy's familiar, hurried handwriting takes up only a small portion of the blank page. I read the only words written on it. "Number one," I read aloud. "Make Gina fall in love with me.

She thinks she hates me. But she'll fall in love with me, even if it's by accident."

A surge of warmth floods through me, carrying an overwhelming mix of beautiful emotions. I turn to face Randy, who is beaming with a hopeful, mischievous smile. His hand rests openly on my thigh, an invitation. I place my palm in his without hesitation. As we gaze into each other's eyes, a profound certainty fills me—it may have started as an accident, but Randy and I are deeply, irreversibly in love.

Epilogue

6 1/2 MONTHS LATER

I GROAN, unable to keep myself asleep any longer. Today was exhausting. I knew I shouldn't have been on my feet for so long, but there was so much work to be done, especially ensuring that the kitchen in the new bakery section of The Calypso was set up correctly.

Yes, Randy insisted on incorporating a bakery—my bakery—into The Calypso's new floor plan. I was hesitant at first, not wanting him to make such a big decision just because I was his pregnant girlfriend. However, he was determined. We went back and forth until he kissed me on the tip of my nose and presented his final argument: he wasn't adding the bakery solely out of love; it made sound business sense to do it, given the popularity and revenue generated by my pastries. How could I counter that? He had won the debate.

But yesterday, I think I overdid it. I'm still extremely sleepy, yet the relentless cramps stabbing into my stomach force me awake. I have to sit up or do something to ease the discomfort. Just as I begin to gently move Randy's hand away from my rounded belly, I notice something alarming. Our bedsheets are wet.

"Oh no," I whisper, realizing what's happening. This is it! The scariest moment of my life has finally arrived, and now that I'm fully awake, the pain is excruciating.

"Randy!" I shout at the top of my lungs.

"What?" he exclaims, startled awake.

"It's time. I'm having Jeffrey!" We decided months ago to name our son after Randy's father.

"All right then," Randy says, his voice steadier now as he calmly gets out of bed and moves methodically through the room.

I'm grateful that Randy is such a calm presence, always able to handle situations with a cool head.

With my birth bag slung over his shoulder, he helps me to my feet, looks me in the eyes, and asks, "Do you remember your breathing?"

Bobbing my head and sucking up the pain, I manage to chirp, "Yes."

"And your pain-management training?" he asks.

"Um-hmm." I grimace as another wave of intense cramping rips through me.

The pain is so intense that I feel almost detached from my body. Despite all the Lamaze and birth pain tolerance classes we've attended, nothing could have truly prepared me for the torment I'm enduring now. This is the ultimate reality check. I was told that Randy and I would be a team during this time, that I would need to rely heavily on him to coach me to the point where I could receive treatment to alleviate my agony—at four centimeters dilated. Until then, I need to trust that Randy remembers our training. Otherwise, all our preparation will have been for nothing.

Thankfully, his head is in the game, and he gets us to the car. As each contraction hits with brute force, he is there, reminding me to breathe deeply and focus on thoughts far removed from the pain.

As I grip the car seat tightly, my thoughts drift

to the happier times since Randy and I officially became a couple. We've gone on so many dates that some might consider it over the top, but Randy wanted to compensate for all the times he held back from asking me out. Each memory serves as a brief escape from the relentless agony, reminding me of the happiness and love that balance out these challenging moments.

"What's on your mind besides what you're feeling, babe?" Randy asks gently, careful not to mention the pain directly, as we agreed he wouldn't use the "*P* word."

"Our dates," I manage to say, my voice shaky from the contractions.

"Tell me about them," he encourages, trying to distract me.

I take a deep breath and begin recounting our memories. "Our favorite dates have to be our walks at noon through the park. We talk about everything—current events, favorite spices, what I loved about studying law, and even the parts I didn't like. No topic is off-limits." I smile faintly, feeling a brief respite as I immerse myself in the recollections. "I know everything there is to know about you, Randy Thorn, and you know me just as well."

I pause, catching my breath, and then continue. "We even made our own bucket lists, remember? We decided to write them separately but promised that each of us would take on the other's list. That way, we have double the adventures to experience together."

As I moan through another contraction, Randy stays quiet, but I can feel his happiness radiating from the gentle way he holds my hand. Sharing those memories does help, if only a little, and right now, I'll take any relief I can get as a win.

"We're almost there," he assures me gently.

"Are we?" I complain, my voice laced with pain and frustration. It feels like we've been driving for hours, even though it has only been a few minutes.

"Tell me more about what makes you happy?" he prompts, eager to keep my mind off the discomfort.

"You," I say, the word carrying more weight and warmth than I expect. "You're a whiz in both Calypso's and our kitchens. I've never been so happy as I have been since the day I moved in with you—and every day after. I love the in-depth tours you've given me, where you share memories from your childhood. I love that you feel comfortable enough with me to cry when a memory hurts, and that my hug can make you feel better."

"Ah, Gina." Randy's voice catches, thick with emotion. Then he takes my hand and gently kisses the back of my knuckles—a gesture he's fond of and often repeats. It's a sweet, loving act that never fails to remind me how deeply he cares.

Relief washes over me as the contraction eases, and just then, we arrive at the hospital. The moments that follow feel like a blur, each one more surreal than the last. Throughout the labor, I cling to every happy memory I can muster, revisiting them repeatedly to help me endure the intense process of giving birth. The pain is nearly overwhelming, but Randy's unwavering presence is my anchor. He stays by my side constantly, helping me move around the room, distracting me from the pain, and coaching me through each phase of labor.

And finally, after what seems like an eternity, I reach a critical milestone—I'm at four centimeters dilated!

"We made it, babe," Randy exclaims excitedly, cradling my sweat-drenched face in his hands. Despite the intense ache that makes it feel like my insides are tearing apart, my heart flutters with love when he plants a gentle kiss on my lips.

Now, finally, the medical staff administers the epidural.

---

2 MONTHS LATER

I must admit that I'm experiencing separation anxiety. I haven't left Jeffrey's side since he was born. He's just so beautiful and precious. His eyes are large and alert, seeming to catch and understand everything we do and say.

Jeffrey hardly cries. Concerned, I even asked Dr. Haskell to give him a thorough check-up because I've heard that babies usually cry a lot, both at night and during the day. But Dr. Haskell, along with my mom and dad, assures me that our son is just fine.

"Babies cry to communicate, Gina," my mom explained. "And you don't miss a beat. Not yet. But one day, you might, and it's okay if you do." Then she patted me on the shoulder and added with a wry smile, "Just don't drop him on his head like I did with you. Several times."

"Ha, ha, ha," I responded with a mock laugh.

Faye Emerson loves her jokes, and even in moments of worry, she knows how to lighten the mood with her humor.

Perhaps this is that moment where I'm missing a beat, because Jeffrey is with my parents, and Randy and I are out on our first date since I delivered the baby.

Randy is nervously tapping his fingers on the steering wheel, and honestly, I find his anxiety reassuring.

"You're nervous about leaving Jeffrey too?" I ask.

Smiling, Randy lets out a soft chuckle. "He'll be fine, babe. But yeah, it's hard being away from him." He glances at the time on the console. "He'd be falling asleep on me right here by now." Grinning nostalgically, Randy pats his left chest.

I throw my hands up. "Let's just make dinner at home, then! Or at my parents' house since Jeff is already there."

Randy squirms in the driver's seat as he considers my suggestion. I'm fully prepared for him to try to convince me to stay out for our adult date night, but instead, he nods enthusiastically. "Okay. Let's just swing by the Calypso and grab some receipts. I have to tally what I owe Jonathan." Jonathan is the construction manager.

BEAMING, I SMILE FROM EAR TO EAR. "YES. OKAY. Thank you, babe."

He winks at me. "You're welcome," he responds cheerfully.

As we pull into the Calypso, I notice that the parking lot is deserted and the inside is shrouded in darkness.

"You want to go in with me and see how things have progressed?" Randy asks.

"Absolutely," I reply eagerly, hopping out of the car to step back into the place where Randy and I fell in love.

Next Monday marks the official reopening of the restaurant. All the staff are returning, except for Sarah, who has moved to Connecticut as planned to run an apple orchard. We've arranged to buy all our apple products from Brimfield Organic Orchards, her new business. I'm looking forward to crafting fresh apple pastries. Sarah has already sent over plenty of product samples, and everything they make is simply delicious.

I'll be back in the bakery one month after

Calypso's grand reopening, as all the empty nesters who lunch insist. "You have to keep it moving after having a baby," Joyce advised me last week. I could almost hear her finger snaps through the phone. She called because it has been two months already, and she thinks I should get back to podcasting. "You young girls. I was back at work in a month."

All I said to her was, "Thank you for the advice, and I'll talk to you later." She can be so annoying, yet for some odd reason, I find myself missing her.

As Randy and I walk toward the doors of Calypso, he holds my hand, and I snuggle into him. "You always smell so good," I remark, rising onto my toes to kiss him on the cheek. Just as I lean in, he turns, and my lips meet his instead.

"Umm..." I hum as we stop to softly smooch.

He arches an eyebrow suggestively. "How about I take you on the couch in my office like old times?"

"How about it?" I purr, so ready. After our six weeks of no sex expired, we've been doing it like rabbits. This time, we've been making love responsibly, of course. Neither of us is ready for a second child—not yet, at least.

Now we rush to get inside, pausing for another quick kiss before entering. Then we step through the doors. I'm eager to see the place fully lit. Everything smells new, and even in the dim light, the place looks freshly renovated. Suddenly, for reasons I can't fathom, Randy drops to one knee.

"Gina?" he says, his voice thick with emotion.

Looking down, I see him holding a diamond ring nestled on a pink silk cushion inside a velvet box. Tears fill my eyes as I realize what's about to happen.

"Randy?" My voice breaks, even before he asks.

"Will you be my forever? My wife? Will you marry me?" he manages to say.

My throat tightens, overwhelmed with emotion, and all I can do is nod vigorously until I finally whisper hoarsely, "Of course."

At that moment, the lights suddenly flash on, and a chorus of "Congratulations!" fills the air. The entire dining room is alive with the people we love —my parents, our baby, and our friends, including Naomi and Derek, who have come in from Boston. Sarah and Dan are in from Connecticut. Even Jeremy and Steve are here. I take a moment to really look at Steve. The color has returned to his skin, and there's a new vitality in his eyes. Randy is hopeful that this time around, Steve will maintain his sobriety. It's a constant effort to stay healthy and happy as a family, but Randy, Jeremy, and now I, are all committed to supporting him.

Steve catches my eye and winks. Smiling, I blow him a kiss. The room is filled with everyone we care about. It's a heartwarming scene, a perfect circle of love and support.

And in this perfect moment, with all our loved ones around us and a future filled with promise, I feel certain that Randy and I are on the path to a happily ever after.